WITHDRAWN

DOCTOR·WHO

The Last Dodo

DOCTOR·WHO

The
Last
Dodo

JACQUELINE RAYNER

2 4 6 8 10 9 7 5 3

Published in 2007 by BBC Books, an imprint of Ebury Publishing.
Ebury Publishing is a division of the Random House Group Ltd.

© Jacqueline Rayner, 2007

Jacqueline Rayner has asserted her right to be identified as the author
of this Work in accordance with the Copyright, Design and Patents Act
1988.

Doctor Who is a BBC Wales production for BBC One
Executive Producers: Russell T Davies and Julie Gardner
Producer: Phil Collinson

Original series broadcast on BBC Television. Format © BBC 1963.
'Doctor Who', 'TARDIS' and the Doctor Who logo are trademarks of the
British Broadcasting Corporation and are used under licence.

The Random House Group Ltd Reg. No. 954009.
Addresses for companies within the Random House Group can be found
at www.randomhouse.co.uk.

A CIP catalogue record for this book is available from the British Library.

ISBN 978 1 84607 224 6

The Random House Group Ltd makes every effort to ensure that the
papers used in our books are made from trees that have been legally
sourced from well-managed credibly certified forests. Our paper
procurement policy can be found at www.randomhouse.co.uk.

Creative Director: Justin Richards
Project Editor: Steve Tribe
Production Controller: Alenka Oblak

Typeset in Albertina, Deviant Strain and Trade Gothic
Cover design by Henry Steadman © BBC 2007
Printed and bound in Germany by GGP Media GmbH

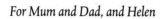

For Mum and Dad, and Helen

Mauritius, 1681

The grunting things had killed her baby. It wasn't the first time: they'd killed her first baby, too, thirty moons earlier, before it had even been born. Their trampling feet destroyed everything in their paths, and babies all around had succumbed to the same casually cruel fate.

She couldn't remember a time before the grunting things had come to her home, but even over her own relatively short life they had become greater and greater in number, while her own kind had become fewer and fewer. The grunting things ate their food and had many, many babies of their own, which would grow up to kill more babies and eat more food. Now, in desperation, her kind had left the home that she somehow knew had once been theirs alone, and travelled to a small, sandy spot which was separated from the grunting things by water.

They thought they were safe. But still, they were all old. There were no more babies.

And one day, death visited again. Not the grunting things; this time death was taller, more colourful, more varied in its shrieks and shouts. Death waited till the water was low, as it sometimes was, and came at them from their old home. At first, she stood around watching, not knowing what was happening, not knowing what these new creatures were. Then suddenly the death-bringing animals ran at them and, too late, she realised that she must run too. She ran, they all ran, but more of the tall things appeared behind them. One of the creatures grabbed her mate and he cried out in fear; she hurried towards him, desperate to help but not knowing how. Others came forward to help, too.

The colourful creatures took them all, all but her. Her escape was sheer luck: the tall things near her grabbed her fellows and none had room left to take her; she was the only one who slipped away.

Still she lingered, for a second, thinking of the mate with whom she had stayed for so many moons, always hoping that more children would come, eventually. But once more she detected his cry, and knew it was the last she would ever hear of him. All around, the tall things were hitting her fellows with boughs from the dark trees, and the noises they made were like those of her baby as it fell beneath the feet of the grunting things. She was so scared. She ran.

She ran and ran, past the tall things, past the places that she knew well, till there was nothing but water before her and she could run no longer. Slowing, she took another step or two forward, but retreated quickly as the brine washed her feet. She turned, hoping against hope to see a companion, but there was nothing but sand, stretching out all around, and the occasional pigeon fluttering round the occasional tree. Had her kind been able to fly like that pigeon, perhaps death would not have claimed them. She felt a hollow resentment at what might have been.

For a few minutes she waited, then she raised her head. Caution battled for a moment with the terrible fear of being alone, and then finally she let out a cry of desperation, a plea for any other of her kind to find her, save her from this fear, this dreadful isolation. But there were no others to hear.

And then more tall ones arrived: two of them, their bodies the colour of the leaves behind which the pigeon was now perching. She had not seen them approach – perhaps they too had swooped down from the sky.

She was tired, so tired, and scared, and hopeless, but still she tried to run. It was no good. The leaf-animals were both calm and fast, and seemed to be in front of her whatever way she turned. Suddenly she felt pressure round her waist, and she was raised from the ground. This was it; this was when she went the same way as her babies and her mate – but she didn't give up, she desperately tried to turn her head, knowing her giant beak, hooked and sharp, was her greatest weapon against these soft, fleshy creatures.

Had she been less scared, she might have realised the difference between the gentle, soothing noises these creatures made and the harsh, cruel cries of the death-dealers. But fear had consumed her now.

One creature said: There's no need to be scared.

The other creature said: We're not going to hurt you.

The first said: I'm sorry. I'm so sorry about what's happened. But at least we can save you.

He lifted a small, square device that was like nothing she had ever seen before, and held it before her.

And the last of the dodos knew nothing else for 400 years.

ONE

Hello, Martha here! Question time for you. Tell me, do you have someone who's your best friend? Someone you thought was great from the minute you met? Someone you have such fun with? I mean, I'm not saying they have to be perfect. But they're pretty much everything you want in a friend. You laugh a lot when you're together – good laughter: laughing with, not laughing at. He's not mean, you see, never mean. And he cares about you, that's important. (By the way, I'm not saying your friend has to be a he. A she will do. Or, as I'm learning as I travel the universe, an it. But my friend, the one I'm going to be talking about when I get on to specifics in a minute, he's a he.)

Where was I? Oh yes, do you have someone, blah de blah de blah etc. Because, as I just revealed (although you'd probably guessed already), I do. I haven't known him very long, actually, not that that's important. But this is the real question: have you ever upset your friend, someone you thought was unupsetable (that's not really a word, but you know what I mean), not in the middle of a row or anything like that (even the best of friends have rows sometimes) but totally out of the blue? Because I just did that. And I wondered what you did to make it up to your friend, especially if you're not even sure what you did wrong.

It might help if I told you what happened. Don't get too excited, it's not like it's a huge drama. In fact, it's a tiny, tiny little thing. Maybe that's the point. Sometimes it's the little things that are worse.

He's a smiley sort of person, my friend (he's called the Doctor, by the way – yes, I know that's not really a name. But you get used to it), and like I say, we laugh a lot. And enthusiastic! He loves everything. He gets excited at all sorts of things, and what's brilliant is he makes you see how exciting they are, too.

Oh, I have to tell you something else, or none of the rest of it will make sense. The Doctor and I, we travel together in a ship called the TARDIS. It's bigger on the inside than the outside, and can go anywhere in time and space. *Anywhere.* I wouldn't blame you if you didn't believe me, but, well, it's true and that's all there is to it.

'Anywhere' is such an enormous concept, though. Sometimes it can be a bit too much. Try to imagine this: your mum says to you, would you like an apple or a Milky Way? I'd usually say 'an apple, please' (no, really, I love apples), but some days I might say, 'Ooh, a Milky Way, thank you', because I felt in a bit of a chocolatey mood.

Now imagine this: your mum says to you: would you like an apple, or an orange, or a pear, or a peach, or a plum, or a pomegranate – and she goes on to name every sort of fruit in the world. And then she says, or a Milky Way or a Bounty – and she goes on to name every sort of chocolate bar in the world. And *then* she says, or maybe a piece of Cheddar, or Caerphilly, or Stilton, or some toast, or a bowl of porridge, or some blancmange, or some pickled-onion-flavour crisps – and she goes on to name *every sort of food in the world*. (Yes, I know that would take days. But we're imagining here.) And you have to pick *just one* and you have to pick it *now*. Your brain would explode with the choice!

I don't know what you'd do, but in an effort to stop the explosion I'd probably grasp at the most familiar, easiest option there was – and say, 'an apple, please'.

The Doctor didn't offer me a choice between every food in the world (actually, for some reason he keeps trying to feed me chips – healthy way to go, Doctor!), what he said to me was, 'Where would you like to go now? I can take you anywhere! Anywhere at all!' There he was, poised over the controls, grinning at me, fingers itching to press the switches that would take me to the place I wanted to go.

I could choose to go anywhere at all. Any house, city, county, country, continent, planet, solar system, or galaxy in the universe. At any time, from the Big Bang to the Big Crunch.

As my brain exploded, I found myself seeking solace in the comfort of childhood, and as if from a distance I heard myself saying the same thing that I always said when I was little and it was the summer holidays and Mum asked me 'Where would you like to go?' I said, 'Let's go to the zoo.'

And the Doctor looked at me as if I'd just kicked his puppy.

No, really, his face kind of fell. Disappointed, but hard at the same time, like he was angry with me. Then his expression relaxed and he just said, in his normal voice, 'Nah, gotta be somewhere better than that. I'm offering you anywhere in the universe!'

So I said, 'Can I think about it?' and he nodded but told me not to take too long, because he didn't want to be wasting time when we could be having fun.

Now I'm wondering what to do, because I know I upset him, but I don't know why. Not only have I still got to choose between the Milky Way and the porridge and the crisps and the other billion options (minus apple), but I have to decide whether to talk to him about it or not. I don't want to upset him again.

If it's ever happened to you, what did you do?

And really, what on Earth is wrong with going to the zoo?

Martha walked into the control room, and found the Doctor sitting in a chair, reading some book with a picture of a rocket on the cover. How he could bear science fiction when he knew what it was really like out there she didn't know – perhaps it amused him, like the way she had begun to find medical dramas hilarious after she started at the hospital. Not that she'd caught the Doctor hanging around reading very often; he wasn't really the sitting type, manic movement was more his sort of thing – she guessed he was waiting for her to tell him her choice, her golden ticket destination, and the instant she did he'd spring into action, pulling levers and pumping pumps and pressing buttons and darting all over the place like he'd got ants in his pants. Fleas on his knees. Eels at his heels.

'Aha! Martha! Excellent!' he said. 'Decided yet?'

She shook her head. 'I didn't mean to upset you,' she said.

He blinked, pretend-baffled. 'You didn't upset me.'

'Yes, I did. But I didn't mean to. Just tell me, so I don't do it again, what's wrong with going to the zoo?'

He frowned at that, seeming to weigh up the options. Finally he simply said, 'Just not really me.'

'Come on, I can tell it's more than that.'

The Doctor sighed and drew in a deep breath. 'OK. It… hurts. The thought of anything being caged hurts me.'

Martha perched on the edge of his chair. 'Oh, but there're plenty of places without cages these days. My these days, I mean, where I come from. They give the animals loads of freedom.'

'Cages don't always have bars, Martha,' he said. 'Just because you call something freedom, doesn't mean it is.' He looked at her, a bit pityingly. For a second she felt angry, patronised, and then something in his eyes suddenly made her understand.

'You couldn't live on only apples and Milky Ways,' she said, slowly. 'You might not starve, but it'd still be cruel.'

The Doctor raised an eyebrow. 'Hungry? I can offer you a thirty-course banquet in Imperial Japan, a kronkburger on Reblais Beta, dehydrated protein tablets on a shuttle to Mars – or there's always chips, nice little chippie in south London…'

He reached forwards, angling for a feather lying on top

of the huge central console, but his fingers only skimmed it. She jumped up to get it for him. It was just a feather, grey and white, nothing to look at twice.

'Seagull?' she asked.

'Bookmark,' he replied, slipping it in place and slamming his book shut with a ringing thud. 'Oh, right, see what you mean. No, dodo.'

Martha stared at him for a second. Sometimes the 'anywhere in time and space' bit took her by surprise in the most unexpected ways. Reblais Beta in the 150th century, fine, animal extinct for three hundred-odd years, her time, unbelievable.

'That's where I choose!' she said, suddenly excited. 'Please? To see a dodo! In its natural habitat,' she added hurriedly.

The Doctor seemed happy enough with her choice. 'Okey dokey, all aboard the good ship TARDIS for a trip to the island of Mauritius – let's say sometime in the sixteenth century, before human discovery, back when the dodo was as alive as… as a dodo.' He was at the controls now, twiddling dials – then suddenly he nipped back over to his chair, picked up the book and opened it again, extracting the dodo feather. He looked hard at his place, said, 'Oh, I expect I'll remember where I was. Can't bear it when people turn over the page corners, just can't *bear* it,' shut the book again, and then was back at the console, inserting the feather into a little hole Martha could have sworn hadn't been there before. The feather stuck out at a jaunty angle like it was on a Robin Hood hat, anomalous but still somehow completely at home among the alien technology.

'That,' said the Doctor, 'will tune us in. Land us right at

their big scaly feet. Sort of automatic dodo detector.' He paused. 'Automatic dodo detector. I ought to patent that, next time we go somewhere with a… what d'you call it? Place where you patent things.'

'Patent office?' Martha offered.

'Good name, like it. You should trademark it. Next time we go somewhere with a… what d'you call it? Place where you trademark things.'

'I don't think there is an actual place—' Martha began, but the Doctor wasn't paying attention.

'Here we go!' he cried. With a final flick of a switch, the TARDIS sprang to life, as excited as its owner to get going once more. Martha fell back into the Doctor's chair as the room began to vibrate. Good job she didn't get seasick.

The Doctor, as usual, seemed oblivious to his ship's eccentricities. He picked up the book once again and swayed over to an inner door, calling, 'Going to put this back in the library. Can't bear books lying around all over the place, just can't *bear* it.'

'But you haven't finished it yet,' Martha called after him. He didn't seem to hear. She wondered how many books he'd never got to finish. She wondered how many books he'd read, full stop. Probably more than existed in the biggest library on Earth.

By the time the Doctor returned, the TARDIS had settled down a bit, although the rising and falling of the column in the centre of the console showed that they were still in flight. The Doctor had swapped his thick paper-paged book for a slim plastic slab, a bit like a large iPod. He held it out to Martha.

She took it, and looked at the screen. 'The I-Spyder Book of Earth Creatures,' she read. 'What's this, then?'

The Doctor grinned. 'Lists every Earth animal there's ever been. You get points for each one you spot. When you've got enough points, you send the book in to the Big Chief I-Spyder, and he sends you a certificate. Thought you could start with the dodo. Quite a lot of points for that one, cos it's only found in such a tiny spot, both spatially and temporally.'

It only took Martha a few seconds to get the hang of the little electronic book. She accessed the index first, but rapidly decided that browsing wasn't the best way forward – 'It's got about 18 billion entries under "A"!' 'Wait till you get to "S",' said the Doctor, 'sandpiper, spiny anteater, seventeen-year locust, Sea Devil…' – and just inputted the word 'Dodo'. A page sprang to life before her eyes: The I-Spyder Book of Earth Creatures: Dodo, *Raphus cucullatus*.

'You get eight hundred points for spotting a dodo,' she noted. 'How many do I need for a certificate?'

'Um… nine million, I think,' he said.

'Oh well. Gotta start somewhere.'

The TARDIS began shuddering again.

'Here we are!' the Doctor announced. 'One tropical paradise, palm trees and non-extinct birds included in the price. Incidentally, here's an interesting if disputed fact: the word "dodo" is a corruption of the Dutch "doedaars", meaning fat, um, rear. So if a dodo asks you if its bum looks big, probably tactful to fib.'

The instant that the ship had ground to a halt, the Doctor's hand was on the door lever. Martha loved that about him, the eagerness to explore, to tear off the wrapping of each new place like a child with its presents at Christmas.

The doors opened. Framed in the doorway was a large browny-grey-y-white-y bird with a little tufty tail and a comically curved beak, far too big for its head. Actually, it was the thing's size overall that surprised Martha the most – she'd been expecting maybe a turkey, and it was much bigger than that, perhaps a metre in height.

But what shouldn't have surprised her was that despite its unbelievably sophisticated technology, despite the Doctor's supposedly expert piloting and despite the automatic dodo detector, the TARDIS had got it wrong again. Oh, a dodo had been detected all right, there was the proof right in front of her. But what it wasn't surrounded by was a tropical paradise complete with palm trees. Instead there was a sign: *Raphus cucullatus*, Dodo. And there was a resigned dullness in the creature's eye.

It was in a cage.

DODO

Raphus cucullatus

Location: Mauritius

The flightless dodo bird is the largest member of the pigeon family and is found only on the island of Mauritius in the Indian Ocean. Its most notable feature is the large, curved beak that dominates its featherless face. It is browny-grey in colour, with curly grey tail feathers and yellow tips to its small wings.

Addendum:

Last reported sighting: AD 1681.
Cause of extinction: hunting by man; introduction of non-indigenous species, e.g. pigs, leading to destruction of eggs and competition for food; destruction of habitat.

I-Spyder points value: 800

Creature	Points
Dodo	800
Subtotal	800

TWO

Martha here again, hello. So, we've found a dodo – and it's in a cage. Of course, that was the last thing I wanted. Well, not the very last, that would be to find ourselves back on the planet Belepheron, where the air smelled of bad eggs and boiled cabbage, and the natives' idea of a friendly greeting was to smother you in green slime and cook you slowly over a fiery pit – look, you know what I mean. We'd just had that really awkward thing about zoos and cages, and I didn't want to go there again, so discovering that the TARDIS had taken us to a bloomin' bird behind bars was not a good thing.

If you'd been there, seeing what I saw, you'd probably ask why I thought it was a captive, not a dead specimen. Why I thought it was alive. For a start, it actually wasn't in a cage, you see, that was just the impression I got at first. It was in a sort of perspex box, the metal bars were part of a floor-to-ceiling grille that spanned the whole room. But the big thing was, it didn't move. Not a millimetre. Not the tiniest flick of a feather. Frozen, it was. Stuffed, you'd probably think. And I don't know why I didn't think that, but I knew it was alive, just knew it. Maybe it's something to do with my medical training – I've seen people slip from life to death with no outward sign at all, and I haven't needed flatlining monitors to tell me what's happened. It's just something about them.

When I could tear my eyes from the dodo, I looked around me and was pretty much staggered. There were these see-through boxes as far as the eye could see, and every box held an animal. I'm not going to start trying to list them, or even describe them. Some boxes as large as Buckingham Palace, some as small as a flea, each with a single creature inside it. That's as far as I'll go at the moment. Maybe more later. Almost certainly more later. But not now, because it's too hard to get my head around it. Just accept that I was stunned. No, what did I say before – staggered. That suits it better.

This sudden realisation, this comprehension of my surroundings, took only a second. I had this momentary thought of shutting the TARDIS doors before the Doctor could see, before he could get upset – but of course even that one second's delay was far too much. I don't doubt he'd taken it all in, probably taken in seven times as much as me in half the time. He was already walking forwards, a grim look on his face.

Together, we stepped out of the TARDIS. And, what do you know? An alarm went off. That's our life, that is.

'Er, back inside the TARDIS is looking a good option right now,' Martha said anxiously, as the siren wailed around them.

'Oh come on, Martha, this is the good bit!' replied the Doctor, not even looking back as he pulled the TARDIS doors closed behind him.

She sighed. 'Oh well, in for a penny... So your plan is, we stay here and be captured or interrogated or whatever by whoever set up that alarm system.'

'Oh yes,' the Doctor agreed, nodding. 'Especially now those guards have turned up.'

He nodded over to their left, indicating the men who were approaching. They looked rather like the security guards from the hospital, with their navy-blue uniforms and peaked caps, but, to Martha's deep discomfort, carried some form of chunky black space gun in their hands – something that the security guards back home had never done, although she thought some of them would have enjoyed it rather a lot.

'Stay right where you are,' one called.

'Whatever you say,' the Doctor called back cheerfully. 'How about we put up our hands too? Would that be a help? Save you having to ask—'

'Shut up!' yelled one of the guards.

'Oh, right, yes, didn't think of that one—'

'Shut up!'

The Doctor raised one hand, and used the other to put a finger to his lips. 'Shhh!' he hissed to Martha, who decided it would probably be a good idea to hold up her hands too.

The men led them out of the room. Martha found it hard to keep her attention on them during the long walk, surrounded as she was by all sorts of bizarre creatures. Her hands kept falling to her sides as she spotted a giant megatherium or a brilliantly plumaged parrot on the other side of the grille, and the Doctor had to keep nudging her to raise them again. He too was paying careful attention to their surroundings, cheerfully pointing out – verbally – a gorilla here and a velociraptor there. Cheerfully, yes – but Martha could see again that hardness in his eyes she'd glimpsed earlier.

As they left the room, Martha turned to see a sign above the door that read, simply, 'Earth'. A logo by its side showed the letters 'MOTLO' in a circle around the head of a strange beast, a line drawing showing tusks and triangular eyes. The emblem was repeated over and over along the corridor they were led down.

'Are we there yet?' the Doctor asked like a petulant child on a car trip.

'Where's "there"?' Martha said.

He shrugged. 'Journey's end. I do hate this low-level threatening stuff that goes nowhere – what good is it to anyone? Let's get into the real stuff, that's what I say.'

'Yes, I can't wait for the real danger to kick in,' she commented drily.

'Good girl,' said the Doctor, grinning at her as the guards came to a halt. 'And it looks like we're getting closer! Excellent!'

Their escorts ushered them through a door, and they passed into a sort of foyer with signs pointing in all directions. Due to the presence of names such as 'Mars' and 'Venus', she assumed the signs referred to planets, although other names were a mystery: Mondas, Refusis II ('I'd like to see those exhibits,' said the Doctor), Varos,

Raxacoricofallapatorius, Tara. She briefly thought there was a planet called 'Gift Shop', until she realised that the sign was indicating, well, a gift shop. This had to be a museum, a gallery, something like that, although one wall displayed a map of continents and oceans, not the floor plan that one would expect in a museum lobby. There was no chance to investigate, however, as the guards led them through a door marked 'No Entry' and they were marched down another corridor. At the end was a door bearing the tusked-beast logo, and they were ushered through it. Martha shivered as she passed inside, temporarily dizzy, although she wasn't quite sure why. Once in the room the feeling passed.

There were no grilles or perspex-boxed creatures here; it was a ludicrously mundane-looking office containing a desk and a chair. On the chair, behind the desk, was sat a woman – a ludicrously mundane-looking woman. Middle-aged, grey-haired, too much red lipstick looking like a clown's mouth against her pale skin. V-necked red jumper with a white shirt underneath and a tweed blazer on top. The whole scene was just so *normal* that Martha felt like laughing – although the still-present guns made her decide it would be a bad idea on the whole.

'Hello!' said the Doctor, springing forward and lowering his arms so he could go for a handshake. 'I'm the Doctor and this is Martha, and we're your prisoners. Which I assume means we've done something wrong, but no idea what. Any clues? Martha? Anyone?'

The woman didn't take the Doctor's hand – they never did, Martha had noted. 'Perhaps you would like to explain,' she said in a low, slightly croaky voice, 'what you were doing in our Earth section outside Northern hemisphere business hours?'

The Doctor reached up and took Martha's left wrist, dragging it down so he could see her watch. 'Martha! Look at that! Your watch must be wrong. It's outside Northern hemisphere business hours and we never realised.'

Martha forbore to point out that the time shown by her watch hadn't borne any relation to the time of her surroundings for quite a while now. The Doctor knew that, anyway.

'Well, sorry about that,' the Doctor continued. 'Glad we've got it all cleared up, perhaps your chums here could put away their weapons now?'

The woman shook her head. 'Oh, I hardly think so. Now you've finally been caught in the act, we're not likely to just let you go. We take theft and sabotage very seriously here at MOTLO.'

The Doctor nodded sympathetically. 'Of course you do. Good for MOTLO. MOTLO, MOTLO, MOTLO. Magic Otters Telephone Lending Office? Magnetic Ointment Treatment Light Orchestra?'

'My Odd Theoretical Love Outlet?' offered Martha, getting a bemused and amused look from the Doctor. ('I am a student,' she reminded him. 'Medical students and bands, you know…')

'The Museum of the Last Ones, as you can't possibly fail to be aware,' the woman told them. 'But perhaps you are not aware that I am Eve, the curator of the museum, and that I have no sense of humour.'

The Doctor looked around the office for another chair,

but, seeing none, perched on the edge of Eve's desk instead. She drew her chair back sharply.

'I'm not after jokes,' he said. 'Actually, I haven't found much funny since we arrived here. Perhaps you could explain why your museum contains living specimens. Perhaps you could explain exactly what your museum is, and what it does. I mean, I wasn't *planning* on sabotaging it, but I could always change my mind. You can help me make that decision. I realise you don't have a sense of humour, but that shouldn't stop you humouring me. What have you got to lose?'

Only the Doctor could sound that threatening and that disarming at the same time.

Eve began to speak. Probably, thought Martha, she wasn't quite sure why she was doing so, why she was obeying the Doctor. After all, logic dictated that two people found in the middle of a building would have a fairly good idea of where they were without needing to be told.

'This is the Museum of the Last Ones,' Eve said again. 'Home to the last remaining specimen of every otherwise-extinct life form in the universe.'

The Doctor blinked. 'But that's trillions upon jillions upon, I don't know, gazillions.'

'And thus the museum encompasses the entire planet,' said Eve.

Martha stared at her. 'Not exactly a family day out, then.'

'More like a year out,' said the Doctor. 'You'd need to pack a fair few picnics. I might be inclined to be impressed, if I wasn't fairly sure I'm not going to like anything I hear.'

'How could you possibly object?' Eve asked. 'This is the

greatest conservation project the universe has ever known.'

The Doctor shuffled around on the desk. 'I knew an old lady who made gooseberry conserve,' he said. 'I don't think there was a lot in it for the gooseberries.'

Eve ignored him. 'We monitor every species, everywhere. When there is a single specimen left, our detectors pick this up. A collection agent is dispatched to retrieve the specimen, so it may be preserved for all time. Thus no species will ever be fully extinct while the museum exists.'

'You expect the last one to just hang around while you bimble down in your rocket ship or whatever?' said Martha incredulously.

The look Eve gave her was extremely pitying. She opened a desk drawer and pulled out a pendant, a chunky metal square on which was a numberpad and a large blue button. 'The collection agents use teleport technology,' she explained. 'They can arrive at the correct location almost instantaneously.' She dangled the pendant tauntingly in front of her. 'But don't think you can use these to escape. Each one is keyed to a specific individual, and will carry that person only.'

'As if we'd try to escape!' said the Doctor indignantly. 'Still, that's not all you use the technology for, is it – I thought I detected a little teleporty swish as we came through your door. That makes sense; being curator of this whole museum would require quite a bit of commuting otherwise. Still, you must work a long day, what with Northern hemisphere business hours, Southern hemisphere business hours, not to mention whatever time they open at the equator…'

'I never sleep,' Eve told him.

'Quite right! It's for tortoises, I always say – unless you're the last tortoise of your kind, of course, in which case you get to be put in suspended animation for all eternity instead.'

'It has to be done,' said Eve. She reached behind her and slid back a wooden panel. Below was a bank of tiny lights the size of pinpricks, hundreds if not thousands of them, flashing in an endless sequence, one after the other. 'Each flash of a light represents an alert,' Eve told them. 'A species has come to an end.'

Martha opened her eyes wide in shock. 'But there have been loads, just since you opened the panel!'

Eve nodded. 'Indeed.'

'The last dodo,' Martha whispered under her breath. 'But, hang on, there was a gorilla there. Gorillas aren't extinct.'

'Martha, Martha, Martha,' said the Doctor. 'Think.'

She thought, and of course it was obvious. 'They're extinct now,' she said. 'Whenever "now" is.'

He nodded sadly. 'I spotted an aye-aye, a Siberian tiger, a chubby little kakapo – puts it a bit after your time, but not necessarily by much.'

Eve was looking both puzzled and fascinated. Martha realised that they had been talking too freely of their bizarre way of life – did they really want this woman to know they were time travellers? – and hastened to dig them out of the hole. 'I left Earth a while ago,' she said. 'Travelling. It's very easy to lose track of time.'

Eve nodded. 'Oh, Earth,' she said. 'I noted you were found in the Earth section. One of our busiest, by far. It wasn't so bad once – the occasional mass extinction every few million years; most planets have those. But in the last few thousand years it's become quite a challenge to keep up with everything that's being lost.'

'Ooh, biting social commentary there,' the Doctor said. 'Not that you don't have a point.' He jumped off the desk. 'Well, thank you for that – glad to have met you, nice to know what's going on, but I think we'll be getting along now. Come on, Martha.'

The guards raised their weapons again.

'Or we could sit here quietly,' continued the Doctor, sitting down again.

'The Earth section,' said Eve, 'is also the site of the recent thefts. All have taken place outside visiting hours. No one has detected the culprit arriving in the museum.' She paused. 'You were in the Earth section. It is now outside visiting hours. Your arrival was not detected until you reached the section itself.'

'I can see your reasoning, Sherlock – not a bad bit of deduction there,' put in the Doctor. 'Wrong conclusion, of course, but…'

'And you appear to have a grudge against our practices. Under galactic law, I have more than enough justification to have you imprisoned pending full investigation by the proper authorities.' She reached out to her computer and pressed a few keys. 'I see we can next expect a justice visit in five months, so until then…' Eve gestured at the guards. 'Take them away.'

'Hang on a minute!' Martha couldn't hide her shock. 'You can't just lock us up for months!'

Eve smiled. 'Oh yes I can,' she said, and turned away.

MOUNTAIN GORILLA

Gorilla beringei beringei

Location: Rwanda, Uganda, Democratic
Republic of Congo

The shy mountain gorilla is a forest-dwelling
herbivore. The male can weigh more than
twice as much as the female. Its fur is black,
although adult males develop silver fur on their
backs, and are therefore known as 'silverbacks'.
The gorilla's arms are longer than its legs. It
walks either on two legs or on all fours, with its
knuckles touching the ground.

Addendum:

Last reported sighting: AD 2030.
Cause of extinction: poached for bush meat
and endangered animal trades; destruction of
habitat.

I-Spyder points: 500

Creature	Points
Dodo	800
Megatherium	500
Paradise parrot	500
Velociraptor	250
Mountain gorilla	500
Aye-aye	900
Siberian tiger	600
Kakapo	900
Subtotal	4950

THREE

A guard grabbed hold of Martha's arm, while another
two pointed their space guns at her. Their fellows were
treating the Doctor in the same way. She threw an anxious
look at her companion – what were they going to do now?

But just as Martha's captor reached the office door, it flew
open, hitting him on the nose. She took the opportunity
to snatch away her arm – although in deference to the still-
raised weapons, didn't try to make a run for it. She looked
instead at the new arrival.

It was a young man – not much older than her – wearing
forest-green overalls with the tusk-headed 'MOTLO' logo
on the chest. He was short, slightly chubby, and sported a
light-brown goatee beard and a worried expression.

'Eve!' he said, ignoring everyone else in his agitation,
'there's been another disappearance!'

The older woman closed her eyes for a second as if
composing herself, and then said, 'What is missing this
time, Tommy?'

37

'The Black Rhino,' the man told her. Eve's lips narrowed but she remained composed – Tommy looked like he was about to cry.

'That makes five,' Eve said, talking more to the air than the man. 'Five irreplaceable specimens. Five creatures lost for eternity.' She turned to the Doctor and Martha. 'If you're expecting any leniency, you can forget it right now. I will be pressing for the maximum penalties the law can offer.'

The Doctor nodded. 'Well, yes, you could do that,' he said. 'Or you could accept that we are innocent and let us help. You see, I happened to notice the Black Rhino as we were being escorted here. It was still there, and still very much alive if far from what I would call well.'

'And you expect me to accept your word for that?'

'Oh, come on – the Black Rhinoceros is twelve feet long and weighs three thousand pounds.' He flung open his suit jacket. 'Search my pockets! Look up my sleeves! If I were wearing a hat you could check under that! And if you're still not convinced, and if you ask nicely, you can even pat down the sides of my legs to check there's not a rhinoceros sewn into the turn-ups of my trousers.'

Eve opened her mouth to speak, but the Doctor started again, gesturing at the guards. 'What's more, considering the absence of one rhino would leave one fairly big empty space, I think your bully boys here would have noticed if its cage was empty when we wandered past on our way out.'

Nervously, the guard with the squashed nose spoke, one hand still massaging his face. 'I saw the rhino,' he said.

The Doctor beamed at him. 'Well observed, that generic guard! Case closed.'

Martha suddenly had an idea. 'Besides,' she said. 'We've actually been sent here to help investigate these... disappearances, and we can prove it.' She stared hard at the pocket where she knew the Doctor kept his psychic paper, hoping he'd get the hint.

'Oh, yes!' he agreed, giving her an appreciative smile and diving into his jacket pocket. 'One set of proof, coming up.'

The Doctor handed over the psychic paper. Martha didn't know how it would appear to Eve, but it would reflect whatever suited the situation best – some sort of identity card or official authorisation.

Or so she thought.

'Is this some kind of trick?' asked Eve, turning the little wallet over in her hands. 'It's blank.'

Ah.

She held it out in front of her. The Doctor, looking just slightly worried, went to take it back, but Tommy intercepted it. He glanced down and then frowned. 'Hang on! This says you're undercover agents with the Galactic Wildlife Trust.' He looked at Eve, confused.

'That's right!' beamed a relieved Doctor. 'Undercover, that's us. In fact, we're under so much cover that even our authorisation papers are shielded in secrecy sometimes.' He snicked the psychic paper out of the man's hand and shoved it back in his pocket before Eve could ask to have a second look. 'So! Now all that's settled, and after these gentlemen have put down their weapons, which I'm anticipating will happen in the very near future, let's get on with some investigating. That's what they pay us for, right, Agent Jones?'

'Right. Yeah. Of course.'

Eve didn't seem precisely happy, but nodded. 'Very well.'

'We could do with all the help we can get!' said Tommy, smiling at Martha. She smiled back. When he wasn't close to tears, he had a very jolly face.

Martha tried to think about the sort of things an investigator would say under these circumstances. 'I'm surprised you haven't set up CCTV cameras,' she tried, adding a bit of disdain to her voice to show the near-arrest hadn't really worried her a bit. 'You know, to keep an eye on things.'

Eve looked at her pityingly. 'We have almost 300 billion species in the Earth section,' she replied. 'Remotely monitoring each one is scarcely practical. We have to rely on movement sensors.'

Martha felt crushed. 'Yeah, but, even so,' she managed.

The Doctor grinned at her. 'Nice try,' he mouthed.

Reassured, she set back her shoulders and had another go. 'Then maybe we should visit the scene of the crime,' she said. 'Er, again. Without anyone arresting us, I mean.'

'A very good idea, Agent Jones,' said the Doctor. 'Better start earning some of that enormous salary that our employers remunerate us with.'

'I'll give you the guided tour,' Tommy announced. 'Earth's my beat.'

'You're a tour guide?' Martha asked him.

He laughed. 'Nope.'

'But Tommy is extremely knowledgeable about the Earth section,' Eve said. 'He was responsible for collecting many of the most recent specimens.'

'Team leader, Earth projects,' Tommy clarified. 'I'm one of the museum's collection agents. Come on, I'll introduce you to the team.'

We left the office and I felt that dizzy sensation again, although this time I knew why: we were being teleported. I think we must have arrived back in a different corridor, because we didn't go through the foyer this time but went straight into the Earth section – entering in a different place meant we really did get a bit of a guided tour before we reached the place where the rhino wasn't, which was fine by me.

Anyway, back a bit, first Tommy introduced us to the Earth team – Earthers, they called themselves. There were six of them altogether, which wasn't as many as I'd expected, but then I suppose even on Earth things aren't going extinct quite that quickly. There was Tommy's partner, Rix, a tall, skinny bloke with big glasses; they looked like a comedy double act. And Rix was definitely the straight man, he barely smiled once. Then there were Vanni and Nadya, another partnership, both about my age and a bit giggly. The last two were Frank and Celia. I was just going to say that Frank was about the Doctor's age when I realised how silly that was – I meant the Doctor's apparent age, sort of mid-thirties-ish, not 900-and-whatever. Takes a bit of getting used to, knowing a Time Lord. So, yes, Frank, mid-thirties, chunky, kept sniffing; Celia, late twenties, bit stuck up. That was the gang.

The Doctor and I smiled, and shook hands, and said how nice to meet them, and Tommy announced we were undercover secret agents, at which the Doctor groaned and shot an exasperated look at the ceiling, but I don't think Tommy noticed that.

I think the Doctor was suffering from a severe case of mixed emotions. On the one hand, I knew he hated this place. Every now and again he would look at an animal, or even just catch sight of the MOTLO logo, and he'd tense up. And I guessed that he'd been as unimpressed by Eve, the boss, as I was.

But on the other hand... well, this whole creature disappearances thing, it was a mystery, wasn't it? And I may not have known the Doctor very long, but I've certainly gathered enough already to realise how he feels about mysteries. Imagine the mystery is one of those enormous cartoon magnets and the Doctor is made of metal and you'll have an idea how he reacts. Clang! The mystery magnet drags him in and he can't resist it.

Anyway, I was telling you about the guided tour. Rix joined Tommy in showing us around. 'Have fun!' called Nadya, as we set off. But fun really wasn't the right word. Well, some of it was fun, like Tommy's joking about (see below), but overall there was just too much awe involved. Tommy and Rix took it in their strides – well, I suppose you get used to even the most incredible stuff after a while – but I just gaped.

Tommy got one of the security men to raise the metal grille so we could wander among the specimens – that's the word he used, 'specimens'; I don't think the Doctor was that impressed, but he put on his polite face and didn't say anything. Tommy was nice, though, don't get me wrong.

What you'd call a 'cheeky chappie'. He made me laugh, although I felt a bit bad about it, because I don't think the Doctor liked that either – Tommy imitating a gorilla, or making fun of the dodo's alleged stupidity. I knew he was thinking it was disrespectful. And it was – but it was still funny. Sorry, Doctor. Sorry, animals.

But I was telling you about the awe. Oh, how can I describe it to you?

You might remember that I briefly met a couple of dinosaurs during a previous time-travelling trip, so you'd think seeing a load of them in cases would be all 'been there, got the T-shirt', nowhere near as impressive. And I'll give you this much: seeing an Apatosaurus lumbering out of the bushes towards you gives you a quiver that a static beast in a museum just can't match. But my 'blink and you'll miss it' encounter hadn't left me as the world's biggest dinosaur expert, and now, being surrounded by them, I started to realise what a big deal it was.

I mean, in my time, there's this huge mystery of what colour the things were – 'no one will ever know for sure,' they used to say, but now I do know – I actually *know* – although to my slight disappointment I can confirm that the guesswork of the illustrators and the model-makers and the special-effects men was right, they're mostly just a dull grey or brown with maybe a bit of green mixed in. I was hoping for some pinks and purples and sunflower yellows, but it was all a camouflage thing, I guess. But there were other things: some had weird feathery bits all over their bodies, some had spines, some had turkey-like wattles or these amazing umbrella frills round their heads, like they were wearing a ruff made out of skin. I could just look around me, and find out all this stuff. I think a palaeontologist would faint with excitement.

That made me curious – did palaeontologists come here? How did the universe work just this little bit into my future? I did this really cunning thing, asking what were some of the latest exhibits and then sneakily looking them up in the *I-Spyder* guide, and I came to the conclusion that we were maybe about sixty years after my time. So, were Earthlings travelling the stars by now, taking it so far in their stride that they could stop off at tourist attractions? I dragged the Doctor to one side and asked him. 'Yes and no,' he said. 'They're out and about a bit, bases on the moon, that sort of thing, a few more ambitious projects, but they're not likely to be popping in here. No organised rocket-coach trips or advertising leaflets through the door; as far as pretty much everyone on Earth is concerned, the dodo is as dead as, the dinosaurs are dinos-aren'ts, and the Indefatigable Galapagos Mouse remains sadly fatigablated.'

That was a bit sad. Although admittedly, after the palaeontologist had recovered from his faint he'd probably find himself out of a job pretty quickly, what with fossils suddenly becoming rather de trop. There's something to be said for things remaining a mystery – what is there left when you know everything?

Not that this was going to be my problem for a while – I can't even remember the names of most of the things I saw, just the famous ones like the stegosaurus and the triceratops, and that was just in this one small area of the museum. I asked Tommy about the Tyrannosaurus rex – really didn't want to see one of those again, OK, so awe and amazement and all that, but meeting one once was about one time too many. Luckily, the museum's 'specimen' was in a section about fifty miles away. Apparently there's a sort of super-speed monorail system to take visitors around, plus a submarine affair for the water-based creatures, but, even so, a visitor could expect to see only a tiny fraction of the 300 billion exhibits, even when some of them were fleas or amoebas or similarly teeny tiny stuff.

Isn't there a theory that people can't visualise any number over – well, actually I can't remember how many, but it's something small like five, or ten. If that's the case, trying to comprehend a number like 300 billion is probably a bit ambitious.

I remember when Mum and Dad used to take us to the zoo as kids, and there were elephants – the type with bigger ears, whichever that is – and probably about four different sorts of monkeys (if we were especially good, Dad'd buy us a bag of monkey nuts to feed them with, and we'd happily stand around for ages watching them nibble at the shells). There was a Giant Panda, that everyone wanted to have babies, and some giraffes. The tiger always seemed to be asleep. That makes… eight. I mean, I expect there were more. Reptiles and birds and things, we weren't so interested in those.

But it makes you think, doesn't it?

Especially when a lot of those 300 billion species are in perspex boxes right next to you and your friend wants to set them all free.

Tommy had pointed out the diplodocus in the distance – at about thirty metres long, it stood out from the crowd

– and was doing a goofy impression of it: 'der, my bwain is so small'. Martha was happily smiling along, when she suddenly realised that the Doctor had dropped behind them. Leaving the Earther laughing at his own joke and digging Rix in the ribs, she slipped away to join her friend. He was looking very grim.

'Sorry,' she said. 'I know I shouldn't laugh. I know you hate it here.'

'Not at all,' he replied, fastening a ghastly false smile on his face. 'As you can see, I'm being nice and normal and friendly, and I shall keep on being nice and normal and friendly, and I shall not go on the rampage or anything, because I try not to do that unless there are lots of monsters around.' He glared at the still-laughing Tommy. 'Although, second thoughts…'

Martha hastily grabbed his hand and dragged him a bit further away. 'It's not monsters,' she said. 'It's something you don't like, and I understand that, but it's not monsters.'

'All these creatures,' he said. 'They're stuck in a living death, Martha.'

'I can sort of see the point, though,' she said, slightly nervously. 'I mean, otherwise these animals would be gone for ever. They've got a dodo! Things that people without a time machine would never see. I know that it's the fault of humans that these animals have gone. We're rubbish. But doesn't this balance it out a bit? Doesn't it undo our mistakes just a fraction – sort of an apology to nature?'

But the Doctor shook his head. 'Ice ages come and go, continents shift, conditions change. Nature didn't intend there to be Ankylosaurus or Dimetrodon in the twenty-first century; they were wiped out long before man first raised a wooden club and said, ooh, last one to kill a woolly mammoth's a rotten moa egg. Do you really think you and your kind would be around today if dinosaurs still walked the Earth? Yes, humans have mocked nature, wiping out the dodo and the passenger pigeon and the thylacine – but this place doesn't apologise, it laughs at her even more.' He drew in a deep breath. 'Better to die free than to live in a cage.'

'The animals aren't aware, though, are they?' said Martha. But she thought how she'd known, known without a doubt, that the dodo was alive, and she wondered if it had been a spark of sentience she had detected.

She looked towards the distant diplodocus, so majestic, so serene, and shivered.

DIPLODOCUS

Diplodocus longus

Location: North America

The giant herbivorous diplodocus is the Earth's longest known land-dweller, more than 25 metres in length. It walks on four legs and has a long, thin neck supporting a small head. Its massive tail – which makes up over half of its length – tapers to a narrow point, and is held horizontal as it walks. It has a ridge of spines down the length of its back.

Addendum:

Last reported sighting: late Jurassic period. Cause of extinction: environmental changes.

I-Spyder points value: 600

Creature	Points
Dodo	800
Megatherium	500
Paradise parrot	500
Velociraptor	250
Mountain gorilla	500
Aye-aye	900
Siberian tiger	600
Kakapo	900
Indefatigable Galapagos mouse	1500
Stegosaurus	500
Triceratops	550
Diplodocus	600
Ankylosaurus	650
Dimetrodon	600
Passenger pigeon	100
Thylacine	250
Subtotal	9700

FOUR

Tommy and Rix finally led the Doctor and Martha to the spot where the Black Rhino had been. Martha had a vague idea that she'd seen a rhino once, but whether it was at the zoo, or a safari park, and if it had been a black one or a white one or a sky-blue-pink one, she had no idea at all. She felt a bit guilty about that. 'You don't know what you've got till it's gone,' she remembered her grandmother used to say, and it was true – probably true of most of the human race.

The see-through box now had a side missing, a big gaping emptiness at the front. The Doctor lost his surly expression, whipped out his glasses and jumped into full-on Sherlock Holmes mode, examining every inch of the outside of the cage, going down on hands and knees to peer closely at the floor surrounding it. Then he went over the inside with a fine-tooth comb, and if Martha thought he'd hesitated just the tiniest bit before climbing in, she'd never have dreamt of mentioning it. Anyway, she'd probably imagined it.

'Any clues, Ace Ventura?' she asked, as he clambered out.

'Apart from the footprints, the cigar ash and the signed confession?' he said.

'Yes, apart from those.'

The Doctor shrugged. 'Not really.' He pointed at a small keypad at the top of the cage. 'I take it that controls the stasis field?'

Tommy nodded. He reached in his pocket and pulled out a white handkerchief covered with little print dinosaurs, which he tossed into the box. Then his fingers dashed out a series of numbers at lightning speed on the keypad. The missing wall shimmered into existence and the descent of the still-floating handkerchief was suddenly arrested; it hung there in mid-air, a snapshot of time.

They stared at the frozen hankie for a few moments, then Tommy reached out and tapped the pad again – Martha mechanically noted the numbers: 5, 7, 9, 3, 1, 0, 0, 8 – and the box's front vanished as quickly as it had appeared; the handkerchief floated gently down to the floor, from where Tommy picked it up and blew his nose noisily.

The Doctor reached up to the keypad. 'No sign of tampering,' he said. 'How many people know the access codes?'

'Just the six of us, the Earthers,' said Tommy slowly, suddenly looking worried.

'And Eve,' added Rix. 'And, really, we've never bothered to keep them that secret.'

'But only the Earthers could switch off the movement sensors,' Tommy pointed out. 'The only time they went off was when you arrived here, Doctor.' Was he only just realising that he and his colleagues were the main suspects, or was it a double bluff to remove suspicion by inviting it so openly?

'Sensors!' the Doctor cried suddenly. 'Why didn't I think of it before? Come on, everyone, we're wasting our time here! Back to Eve's office!'

He dived off, calling 'No time to lose!' over his shoulder. Martha jogged to keep up. 'What is it?' she said. 'What's up? Something about those movement sensor things?'

'Nope,' he replied, not slowing down. 'Not them. Remember that bank of lights? Alerts every time a population gets down to one. Presumably once that creature is in stasis, the alert disappears. But what if it's reactivated?'

Martha 'oh'ed in understanding. 'So once the rhino was removed from stasis, its warning light would come on again.'

'Yup.'

'And if we can track down the rhino, we might be able to find whoever nicked it.'

'Yup.'

Martha thought about it. 'But what if it's dead?'

The Doctor did a running shrug. 'Then this won't work. But it's only been gone, ooh, twenty minutes max? Hope springs eternal, Agent Jones, hope springs eternal.'

The Doctor's unerring direction sense brought them back to the exit, and he raced down the corridor and through the foyer while Tommy, Rix and Martha struggled to keep up. By the time they reached Eve's office, the Doctor had already burst in. Ignoring Eve's obvious disapproval of his unheralded entry, he launched into an explanation of his theory.

Luckily, Eve caught on at once, and her frown vanished. 'I should have thought of that,' she said. 'But the alerts are in chronological order; it never crossed my mind to go back through past extinctions…'

'No time for tears,' the Doctor told her, although anyone who looked less likely to break down crying Martha couldn't imagine. The Doctor ducked behind the desk and pulled back the wall panel to reveal the warning system. He and Eve bent over it as Martha, Tommy and Rix looked on anxiously.

'Yes!' The Doctor looked up, beaming. Even Eve was smiling in delight.

'You've found it?' asked Martha. The Doctor clicked his fingers in mock modesty.

'It's back on Earth,' Eve informed everyone.

'So where do we go from here?'

'We go after it, of course!' said the Doctor. 'Back to good ol' Earth.'

Rix looked slightly taken aback. 'I think that's our job.'

The Doctor flashed him a smile. 'Oh, I think you'll find it's ours too.' He turned to Eve. 'You'll authorise us, I'm sure.'

She nodded, and reached forward to open a desk drawer. From inside she pulled out two of the pendant-like devices and handed one each to the Doctor and Martha, then turned to her computer. 'I'll programme you in,' she said, and then, thirty seconds later, 'OK. All done. Enter these coordinates…'

She reeled off a list of figures, and Tommy showed Martha the buttons on the pendant to press. 'Then it's the big blue one to operate it.'

'Come on then,' said Rix, impatiently.

'Earth ho!' called the Doctor.

As one, he, Martha, Tommy and Rix pressed their blue buttons. As one, they disappeared…

… and found themselves somewhere else.

They were in a gloomy warehouse; bare concrete walls and floors made it seem colder than it was, and the dim strip lighting that was the only illumination didn't help. In a couple of corners lay things that Martha instinctively didn't want to investigate too closely; even her medical training didn't overcome that initial squeamishness on seeing something that was certainly dead, and no longer whole. In another corner lay something more recognisable – what must be the Black Rhinoceros. The Doctor was already moving towards it, and Martha followed him warily.

'Look at you, you're beautiful,' he said softly. Then: 'There's no danger, it's been tranquillised,' he called back as he reached the magnificent creature. But now that hard edge was back in his voice.

'Oh,' exclaimed Martha as she joined him, immediately spotting the problem.

Tommy arrived by her side. 'Its horn,' he said. 'It's gone!' For a second the anger in his expression matched that of the Doctor.

The rhino had once had two horns, a huge, piercing spike that dominated its face, and a smaller, modest one behind that. It was the larger of the two that had vanished, leaving the creature, however giant, now looking forlorn and somehow feeble.

'Sawn off,' the Doctor said, bending closer to examine the stump, crusty with dried blood.

'But why?' Martha asked.

Tommy was no longer the light-hearted joker of earlier; he looked disgusted. 'One of the reasons they became extinct in the first place – idiots getting it into their heads that rhino horn could cure all ills. People'd pay through the nose for it, and poachers would be happy to provide.' He sighed. 'We should thank our lucky stars this one's still alive. The poachers didn't usually take such care.'

Martha shivered, and looked up for the Doctor's reaction – but he'd left the drugged animal and was wandering over to a door on the opposite side of the warehouse. It needed a zap of the sonic screwdriver, but a few seconds later he was through. Martha, feeling that she was spending most of the day following in his wake, trotted after him.

There was a tiny, spartan office through the door, containing nothing but a table, a chair and a computer. The Doctor sat on the chair, wiggled his fingers as if he were about to launch into a piano concerto, and then plunged at the keyboard.

'Notice anything interesting about this room?' he asked Martha, without looking up.

She turned her head. 'Interesting' was not a word she would have chosen to describe her surroundings in any way. There was no other furniture, no decoration, just a barely illuminating fluorescent tube in the ceiling. To her left was a plain wall of breeze blocks, the same in front of her and to her right. Behind her was the door through which she'd entered. *Oh.*

'There's no exit,' she said. 'You can only go back the way you came.'

'And notice anything interesting about the way we came?'

This time it was easy, now she knew what she was looking for. 'There was no exit in the warehouse, either. This was the only door. There wasn't even a window.'

The Doctor nodded. 'Handy if you're doing something dodgy and don't want visitors, don't you think?'

'Perhaps there's a teleport,' she suggested.

'Which wouldn't be native Earth technology at this time,' he told her. 'Yet another indication that it's an inside job, Agent Jones. The museum folk seem happy enough to zap around all over the place. Aha!'

Martha walked round to look over his shoulder and see what he'd discovered.

There was a list of names: Quagga. Bluebuck. Black Rhinoceros. There were a lot more than the five Eve had suggested. Below each name was, first, a short string of numbers and letters, second, a long row of figures. 'What do they look like to you?' the Doctor asked.

She looked at the top row, under 'Quagga': 3.7M. It took a few moments, but she got it. 'Million,' she said. 'The "M" must stand for million. There should be a pound sign or a dollar sign or something in front.'

'And the other numbers?'

Again a few seconds thought, then: 'They're in the same format as the coordinates Eve gave us to get here. But what's a quagga? Some sort of animal, I guess.'

The Doctor looked sad. 'Relative of the zebra, a subspecies – looks just like one, except it's only striped on the head and part of the body, and it's a chestnut-brown colour with white stripes, rather than black and white like a zebra – a quagga crossing wouldn't show up on the road nearly as much, but it was a beautiful animal. Good old humans – they didn't even realise it was a creature in its own right until after the last one had died. In fact, they didn't even realise they'd all died out for years.'

'Killed by humans?' Martha asked, knowing the answer.

'Oh yes, all the ones in the wild, end of the nineteenth century, shot by settlers who thought it might eat up the grass they wanted for their cows. The last known quagga died in an Amsterdam zoo in 1883. Or at least, the last known up till now. Goodness knows where *MOTLO's*' – he said the name disdainfully – 'one came from; hidden in a little corner of South Africa or in some private collection somewhere.'

'And now it's gone too,' said Martha, sadly. Only two minutes ago she hadn't known that this animal had ever existed, and now she knew that it had, and it had been lost, and lost again, and the sudden stab of regret was almost unbearable. 'Sometimes I hate *people*,' she said.

The Doctor grabbed her hands in his. 'Martha! No, no, no! Hate what some of them do, hate some individuals if you must, hate intolerance and injustice and slaughter and man's inhumanity to man, but never, never hate *people*.' He skimmed through the list, pointing out a name here, a name there. 'The Paradise Parrot. The Ilin Island Cloudrunner. Whether or not humans were responsible for their disappearance, what you have to remember is that it was humans who were responsible for coming up with such inspiring, evocative names in the first place.' He threw out a hand. 'The cloudrunner! How brilliant is that? Some human discovers these fluffy rodents skitting about high up in the mountain treetops, and instead of calling them "tree rats" or "mountain mice", they decide to call them "cloudrunners". Don't you feel something stirring inside you when you hear that?' He smiled. 'It's embarrassing, but actually some of my best friends are human.'

Martha couldn't bring herself to smile back, not even at the thought of a cute fluffy rodent; she was finding it hard to marshal her thoughts on such matters just for the moment. She sought refuge in the mystery at hand. 'So... someone's selling off these animals. The quagga and the bluebuck and everything. For whacking great sums. And the coordinates are where they've been taken, the delivery address.'

The Doctor nodded. 'That's exactly what I thought.'

Martha had opened a desk drawer. 'There's a duplicate list in here,' she said. Then she frowned. 'That's funny. Here, the bluebuck's listed as 4.2 million. On the screen –' she checked – 'it's 4.4.'

'Maybe they had a sale,' the Doctor said, in what she considered to be slightly bad taste. 'Prices slashed! Everything must go! If you find an extinct animal on sale anywhere else for less, we'll refund the difference! As long as they don't do a "buy one, get one free"... that could cause ructions.'

Martha gave him a look, and he adopted a falsely contrite expression in return. 'Tell you what, it'll probably all become clear when we investigate. That's an idea! Shall we investigate, Agent Jones?'

She glanced back through the doorway. 'What about Tommy and Rix?'

'Well we could tell the two suspects what we're up to…' He grinned, already programming the first listed coordinates into his pendant. 'But you know what they say, two's company…'

'And four's two too many.' She was copying the figures into her own device. 'Except for the Fab Four… four seasons pizza…'

'The Four Yorkshiremen sketch… The Four Just Men…'

'The Four Tops, the Fantastic Four…'

'Radio 4, the Four Tenors…'

'That's the Three Tenors!'

'Well, yes, it is now, I mean they begged me to join them permanently but I couldn't really spare the time, not with how often I have to save the world… Ready?'

'Ready.'

They pressed their blue buttons.

ILIN ISLAND CLOUDRUNNER

Crateromys paulus

Location: Ilin Island

The Ilin Island Cloudrunner, found in the forests of the tiny Philippine island of Ilin, is a large browny-grey rat. Its distinctive feature is its long furry tail.

Addendum:

Last reported sighting: AD 1953.
Cause of extinction: destruction of habitat.

I-Spyder points value: 2000

Creature	Points
Dodo	800
Megatherium	500
Paradise parrot	500
Velociraptor	250
Mountain gorilla	500
Aye-aye	900
Siberian tiger	600
Kakapo	900
Indefatigable Galapagos mouse	1500
Stegosaurus	500
Triceratops	550
Diplodocus	600
Ankylosaurus	650
Dimetrodon	600
Passenger pigeon	100
Thylacine	250
Black rhinoceros	300
Subtotal	10000

FIVE

Eve had swivelled her chair round so she could access the wall panel more easily. Her head was full of the facts and figures of previous extinctions, and now the Doctor had given her the idea it was easy to check up on the other missing creatures, although their original disappearances ranged over several million years.

There was no trace of the other animals. She looked at the quagga, the bluebuck and the paradise parrot. The lights did not so much as flicker.

But there was another light.

If Eve had been one to doubt her own senses, she might have thought she was imagining it. Even with her self-assurance, she checked it twice.

The light was definitely there.

There should be no other lights. She was utterly, thoroughly, ruthlessly efficient, and she knew that every ordinary extinction had been dealt with.

Every *ordinary* extinction.

Her mission was this: to stop any species from dying out. She had to preserve the last example of each species, and let the universe see them all.

She did her best, did everything she could, but even so there were circumstances which defeated her. Eve had no magical powers to foretell the future; oh yes, she could make logical predictions, and indeed had utilised these to great effect on a number of occasions, but as to *knowing* what was going to happen, that was beyond her skill. So she'd been caught unawares, at times – some unseen disaster befalling a planet, destroying every creature within a fraction of a second, when even the most skilful of computers would have been unable to detect which specimen was the last of its kind and there was no time to send a collection agent to retrieve it, even if it had been identified.

Eve prided herself on being free from emotion, but the sensations that occurred at such times could really be described in no other way. Pain. Regret. Anger. To know that she had failed in her objective, that the collection would never, could never be perfect. But it made her even more determined to succeed in future. Oh, sometimes the universe played tricks, she knew. Take the Daleks, for instance. They'd wink out of existence in the far distant past, then suddenly emerge again as if from nowhere. Their mass extinction had been recorded so many times she'd stopped trying to keep track. But she had other records of their planet, at least. She had specimens from every planet that had ever known life, and that was a consolation to her.

Or it had been. For suddenly there was one planet… Had it happened millions of years ago, billions, last week? Even now, seeing the warning light again, she couldn't pin it down. All she knew was that suddenly, without warning, a planet had been destroyed. Gone forever. The planet had never known an extinction before that, somehow – seemingly magically – even the most fragile of insect species had survived as long as its home. And then – all gone.

All except one. One solitary specimen of one solitary species of all that had existed on that one planet.

And then the one had gone, and with it Eve's consolation. Free from emotion? No, it… hurt.

And something was stirring within her now, something she'd never experienced before. Could it be… desperation? Need? Desire? Or just a certain knowledge that if she did not pursue this, she would remain forever unfulfilled? Whatever it was it was strong, so strong.

Her head swimming with unfamiliar thoughts, she leaned back in her chair and pondered her next move.

I'm getting used to the zappy stuff now. The way I'm dealing with it is this: pretending I've gone on a long train journey, only without the signal failures, the person next to you who takes up half your seat with their bags and tries to read your newspaper over your shoulder, the £17 per biscuit buffet, the lack of air conditioning and, of course, the train journey. That way it seems like a really positive experience, instead of one where you feel sick and dizzy and get freaked out that half your atoms haven't made it, and those that have turned up are in the wrong places. I mean, what if something goes a bit skewy and my ear gets reassembled out of my nose or something? (And, believe me, that's not the worst example

I can think of but you'll have to use your imagination. No, on second thoughts, please don't use your imagination. Just forget all about it. Please.)

Anyway, so we zap away – destination who knows where, but that sort of thing doesn't bother the Doctor – on the trail of who knows what (but he doesn't let that stop him, either).

And where we end up – well, total contrast to the warehouse place. Walls papered in velvet (um, can something be 'papered' in non-paper?), carpets you have to wade through, chandeliers and huge vases and gold bits on everything. And right there with her back to us, a kid in a maid's uniform dusting the knick-knacks. The Doctor coughed and she turned round, saw us and screamed. Two seconds later we were surrounded by what appeared to be armed butlers. Didn't faze the Doctor, of course. There we are, about to be thrown out on our ears – possibly with police arrest to follow and, who knows, maybe a bit of violence on the side – but he just calmly states that we have an appointment with the owner of the house. 'I think not,' says this one posh-suited butler guy, but the Doctor just replies, 'Go on, go and tell 'em we're here. And say "quagga".' He said it like it was a code, and even though I knew how serious the situation was it was hard not to laugh, cos it sounds such a funny word, like 'wibble' or 'bibble'. But the guy obediently vanished, and I can only assume he did what the Doctor asked because a couple of minutes later this woman appears in the doorway, and she's so in control and obviously stinking rich she has to be the person we're looking for.

Besides, we can see right away that she's the one who bought the quagga. And suddenly I feel a bit sick.

'Ooh, nice coat,' said the Doctor, plonking himself down on a spindly chair that creaked under his weight.

It wasn't really a nice coat at all. In style it resembled a biker jacket, cut high on the waist and tightly fitted. It was made of coarse skin, the hairs on it lying flat and glossy, like on a horse's rump. One sleeve and lapel were striped brown and white, the stripes fading to pure brown for the rest of the jacket.

The woman, frowning, gestured for the hordes of servants to leave the room. 'I shall be fine,' she said in a deep European accent, as one or two looked ready to protest.

'Yes, your ladyship,' said one, the butler who had fetched her, and led the rest out of the door.

'You requested an audience,' said the woman, turning to the Doctor and Martha. 'From the manner of your arrival, I am thinking that I know from where you haf come. And yet I was notified of no such visit.'

The Doctor shrugged his shoulders. 'Please accept our apologies.' He waved at Martha. 'Breaking in a new recruit, can't get anything right…'

Martha opened her mouth to protest, and then thought better of it.

'… lowest rung of the ladder, hasn't even met the boss yet – I suppose you were expecting to hear from the boss if you heard from anyone at all.'

The woman gave a disdainful half-nod. 'I do not usually deal with underlings.'

'And I don't blame you, Mrs. But he –' at this, the Doctor stared hard at her expression, but she gave no indication that he was wrong in his assumption – 'had to delegate this time. Pressures of business and all that. After all, in such a multi-million concern…' He narrowed his eyes and let them roam over the woman's body. 'Yes, that coat's well worth 3.7 million, if you ask me. Wouldn't you agree, Martha?'

'It's a bit short,' said Martha critically.

'I hear what you're saying.' The Doctor maintained a look of unconcerned interest. 'But usually a coat is made up from two or three animal skins – large animals, that is – and obviously in this case that just wasn't possible.'

The woman nodded. 'I did consider combining it with the skin of a zebra,' she said. 'But the colours, they would haf clashed, and that would haf diluted the effect, no? Diminished it.'

'Oh, quite. But as it stands, you're happy with it? Happy with the service you received?'

The woman indicated that Martha should sit down next to the Doctor, then took a chair herself. 'Well, it is hard to say. Of course, in many ways the skin is not ideal for the purpose, and perhaps the style is not all it could be—'

'Where I come from,' Martha put in, unable to help herself, 'zebra print is considered a bit trashy.'

The woman looked her up and down, clearly taking in the red leather jacket and silver hoop earrings. 'Ah yes, I see that you come from a place most stylish, most… chic,' she said with one perfectly plucked eyebrow raised. Martha felt her cheeks grow warm.

'But as I was saying, to possess that which no one else

in the world possesses – that is what elevates this above mere style. Skin *qua* skin, it is nothing. But it is so much more. Just to see Lady Horsley's face…' A complacent smile spread across her own face for a moment, then she became businesslike and tossed her hair impatiently. 'But surely this is not just a customer satisfaction survey? I take it that you haf news for me? My next order, it is ready?'

'Oh, the Tasmanian Tiger handbag?' said the Doctor, carelessly.

The woman frowned. 'The what?'

'Sorry, my mistake,' said the Doctor, 'confusing you with someone else. Maybe Lady Horsley.' She looked both worried and furious at that, but he pretended not to notice, just carried on speaking. 'No, actually, this really is more in the line of a customer satisfaction survey. Young Martha here, learning the business like I said, essential that she sees what goes on… I wonder, would you be so enormously, enormously good as to run through the procedure for her, with your opinions on your treatment at each stage?'

She frowned, but gave a short nod. 'You understand, however, that my time is valuable…'

'Oh, quite. Half a million discount for next time, guaranteed.'

A smile, as she turned to address Martha. 'You must first understand, girl, that there is nothing more important in this life than that which is unique. A thing which can be had by anyone – what is the value there? One's superiority must be demonstrated exactly. I own the largest sapphire in the world. The only portrait ever painted by the genius Johann Illes is of me. The—'

The Doctor interrupted. 'Johann Illes? He disappeared, didn't he?'

A lazy, catlike smile spread across her face. 'Sadly true. And just after rumour had it he was planning a portrait of Arabella Horsley…'

The Doctor half rose from his seat, then sank back down again. 'Ah,' he said, then after a moment, 'Do go on.'

She waved a hand. 'I am sure the girl has by now grasped the idea. The quest for uniqueness, however, is never ending, and in the matter of couture it is almost impossible. A one-off by a designer who can be bribed? Pah. The hat of takahe feathers, the komodo leather boots, all can be duplicated by those with money and… efficiency to equal mine.'

'And with an equal disregard for the law and the sanctity of life,' said the Doctor in a polite, friendly and interested way.

The woman – whose name they did not know and could not ask for without arousing suspicion – acknowledged this as simple fact. 'True. But in the circles in which I move – well, that—' she laughed in anticipation of her own joke – 'that, it is *not* unique.'

Martha sat on her hands so she would not be tempted to slap the woman.

'And then a rumour reached me, via my furrier – something was being offered, something unheard of. Something that no other person in the world could possibly possess. And, furthermore, the offer was being made only to me.' She turned briefly to the Doctor. 'Your organisation, they do at least understand the necessity of that. I was less pleased, of course, to hear that the offer would be taken elsewhere if I did not respond. Ah well, I suppose that also shows understanding, a brain of business there. For how could I let such an offer get away? The negotiations, they were long and, I cannot deny, tedious. I had to take a great deal on trust, and perhaps that is something that you could look into, although I admit, perhaps, that such must always be the case when one is in such a… delicate situation. And then, of course, there was the handover of goods.'

'And the boss himself was dealing with you at this point?' the Doctor asked, as if he already knew the answer.

'But of course,' she replied.

'And you were happy with his personal attentions?'

She laughed, puzzled. 'The deal was concluded. I had no reason to complain.'

'He was polite, attentive, all that?'

She looked quizzical still. 'But of course, I never met him. A rumour here, a message there… and then, finally, the… sordid conclusion: a transfer of money and goods in a locked room. This room. I do not know how my money disappeared and the skin arrived, but such they did and I am content. And now, about my next order…'

'Not our department, I'm afraid.' The Doctor's face had sunk, and he jumped from his chair with considerably less enthusiasm than he had possessed earlier. 'Well, we won't bother you any further, time is money, money is giant sapphires and one-off paintings and easy access to murderers and all that, come on, Martha—' She leapt up too, as did the woman. 'We'll see ourselves out, the normal way this time, no need to summon a butler or anything—'

The Doctor had reached the door to the room by now,

and was twisting the handle, squeezing it tight like he wanted to hurt it. 'Oh, by the way,' he tossed carelessly over his shoulder as they left, 'did you know there are twenty-three stuffed quaggas in museums around the world? After all, it's not even been extinct a couple of centuries. Bit of robbery, anyone could have a coat like yours. Lady Horsley, for example. And there's you paying millions for it. Shame. Perhaps that's even where yours came from. Hardly unique at all. You know what they say, there's no fool like a one-off fool.'

Martha looked back at the quagga-robed woman. Horror, surprise and fury mingled on her face. She seemed to be trying to say something, and it seemed to Martha to be a very good idea to get out of there before she managed it.

QUAGGA

Equus quagga quagga

Location: Southern Africa

The plains-dwelling quagga is a four-legged, hoofed mammal related to the zebra. Its coat is striped brown and white on its head and neck, the stripes gradually fading over the course of its body until it is plain brown.

Addendum:

Last reported sighting: AD 1883.
Cause of extinction: hunting by man.

I-Spyder points value: 200

Creature	Points
Dodo	800
Megatherium	500
Paradise parrot	500
Velociraptor	250
Mountain gorilla	500
Aye-aye	900
Siberian tiger	600
Kakapo	900
Indefatigable Galapagos mouse	1500
Stegosaurus	500
Triceratops	550
Diplodocus	600
Ankylosaurus	650
Dimetrodon	600
Passenger pigeon	100
Thylacine	250
Black rhinoceros	300
Subtotal	10000

SIX

The Doctor was adjusting coordinates on his neck pendant, instructing Martha to do the same. 'Probably not wise to stick around,' he said, with which she agreed wholeheartedly.

'Was that true?' she said. 'Could the quagga have come from a museum instead? Been an… already dead one?'

He shook his head, a tense, unhappy gesture. 'Nope. Not really practical, you know, preservatives and all that. But I hope she goes on thinking it for the rest of her life…'

The wave of nausea that kept threatening Martha broke across her stomach again. 'I'm not going to say anything,' she said. 'Cos, like my dad always says, there's no point preaching to the choir. But I don't want to meet anyone like that ever again.'

The Doctor looked at her. 'Shame, that,' he said. 'Because, in case you didn't notice, we didn't exactly pick up a lot of clues there. So we're trying again. Maybe someone will have made a slip. Gotta live in hope. Press your button.'

And, bracing herself for what they might find at the next set of coordinates, she did.

Their next place of arrival was rather a surprise after the opulence of the previous location.

It was a caravan.

It was in a muddy field in what seemed to be the middle of nowhere, and it wasn't even a particularly nice caravan, at least it didn't look so on the outside. It was quite small and bits were falling off it. Thick brown curtains masked the view to the inside, although the windows were so dirty that they probably wouldn't have been able to see much anyway.

The Doctor and Martha looked at each other, and did a synchronised shrug. Then the Doctor knocked on the door. There was a sound from inside like a surprised person going 'eep', but no call for them to enter. The Doctor knocked again, more forcefully. This time there was no sound at all. The Doctor knocked for a third time, and a male voice shrieked 'Go away!'

'No, sorry!' called back the Doctor, cheerfully, trying the door handle. The door was locked.

'We only want to talk to you,' Martha added, in what she hoped was a nice, reasonable, friendly tone, although, after the encounter with the quagga-coat woman, she wasn't feeling particularly reasonable or friendly.

The Doctor was now trying a window. It didn't appear to have a lock and, due to the condition of the caravan, didn't fit properly in its frame. He pushed hard, and it sprang open.

'Isn't this breaking and entering?' asked Martha nervously, as the Doctor pushed aside the brown curtain.

'I haven't entered yet!' he replied. Then he stuck his head through the gap. 'Ooh! Now I have!'

Martha stood on tiptoes and looked through the window too.

There was a table to one end of the caravan. Protruding from under it was a pair of feet, as of a person trying to hide from view but not doing it very well. The feet wore slippers – tartan ones, so at least they weren't made out of some extinct animal, unless it was a very bizarre Scottish one she'd never heard of.

'Hello!' the Doctor called.

'Go away!' the man said again, his voice slightly muffled by the table.

'We're doing a follow-up on a recent… purchase of yours.'

The man's voice, already high, rose up to a screeching panic. 'I haven't bought anything!'

'What, nothing?'

'Nothing!'

'Ever?'

'Ever!'

'Goodness,' said the Doctor to Martha. 'That's taking anti-consumerism quite far. It's also probably not true.' He stretched a hand through the window, leaned awkwardly towards the door, and clicked open the lock from the inside. Glad to get her nose away from the musty curtains, Martha withdrew her head and followed him as he hopped up a tiny portable step and went through the door.

She would have felt guilty for invading this man's privacy if he hadn't been one of the unknown thief's customers;

as it was her heart had hardened. But the man, when he emerged in a backwards crawl from under his fold-down table, seemed about as far from the 'unique' lady as could be. He was short, much shorter than Martha, probably not a lot over five feet tall, and had a fringe of white hair and, when he was finally clear of the table, a face full of white hair too. For a second Martha thought this was some sort of extinct albino weasel attached to his upper lip, but it turned out on closer viewing to be an enormous moustache and extremely bushy mutton-chop whiskers.

'Hello!' said the Doctor, taking a seat on a padded bench out of which springs were sticking. 'I'm the Doctor and this is Martha, and we've come to—' He broke off. 'Hey! Don't I know you?'

The little man shook his head so forcefully that the moustache ends whipped his cheeks. 'I am completely unknown!' he said.

'No, no... yes, that's it, your name's Dunnock!'

'I am not Professor Dougal Dunnock!' protested Professor Dougal Dunnock.

'Professor Dougal Dunnock! Yes, I've seen your picture on a dust jacket. *Fishy Fingers: Evolution from Sea to Land*.'

'I did not write that bestselling and revolutionary scientific treatise!' Professor Dunnock insisted.

Martha blinked in surprise. 'Bestselling? Then how come you're living in a falling-down caravan?' She stopped. 'Sorry, that was a bit rude.'

The old man flung up his hands. 'Well, obviously I had to sell everything I owned in order to buy... nothing,' he finished hastily.

'Nothing. Because you've never bought anything in your life,' clarified the Doctor. Dunnock nodded eagerly. 'No… extinct animals of any kind.'

The professor caught his breath. 'No indeed, sir! Do you mean to imply that I might be hiding some sort of missing link in my bathroom?' He stepped over to an internal door and stood in front of it, making a human barrier. As it was the only internal door, Martha strongly suspected it led to the bathroom – not that there was anywhere like enough room for an actual bath (and, as far as she could judge, Professor Dunnock certainly didn't seem to have been acquainted with an actual bath recently).

The Doctor stood up and, with a foot's height advantage, reached over the little man to push open the door. Dunnock turned and grabbed the door handle with both hands, pulling it shut, but not before Martha had caught a glimpse of a small grey creature a bit like a hairy mudskipper sitting in the tiny sink.

She turned to the Doctor. 'That's the missing link between sea animals and land animals?'

'A missing link, not *the* missing link,' he said. 'It didn't go cod, cod, missing link, badger, badger, or anything like that, the process was rather more gradual. Something Professor Dunnock should know all about, being a world expert on the subject as I seem to recall.'

Dunnock waved a hand deprecatingly, then seemed to remember he wasn't supposed to be Professor Dunnock at all and frowned instead.

'You're not going to dissect it or anything, are you?' asked Martha, a bit worried.

The professor looked startled. 'Dissect Mervin? Of course not.'

'Mervin… the Missing Link.'

'No!'

'Mervin… the not-Missing Link who isn't in your bathroom who you didn't sell all your possessions to buy?'

The little man's head wavered between a shake and a nod.

The Doctor sighed and sat down again. 'I suppose you didn't receive some sort of secret intelligence and set up a clandestine rendezvous to make the purchase, either?'

Dunnock sniffed. 'Do I really look like the sort of person to arrange to meet a strange young man in a dark alleyway to conduct an illicit purchase?'

Martha jumped on this. 'A young man?'

'And you wouldn't remember his name – or what he looked like?' asked the Doctor urgently.

But on this, the professor resolutely refused to deny anything at all.

Finally, fed up, Martha sat down on the bench and sighed. 'I just don't get it,' she said. 'Can I ask, hypothetically, why a hypothetical professor would be keeping a hypothetical missing link in his bathroom and hiding under the table if anyone comes round?'

Dunnock threw his hands in the air. 'My dear young lady, that is precisely the point! Because it is not hypothetical!'

'Well, I know it isn't, but I thought…'

'I think what the not-professor means,' interjected the Doctor, 'is that the "missing link" is no longer a subject for hypotheses, because it is actual.'

'Oh, right,' said Martha, remembering her thoughts about how the museum would be ruinous for palaeontologists. 'You're worried that you'll be out of a job when people don't need to speculate any more.'

'Of course not,' said the professor, who seemed to have forgotten that he didn't know what they were talking about, 'I'm worried that I'll be out of a job if it's discovered that my book – my research, my reputation! – is built on a false premise.' He opened an overhead cupboard and stretched up to reach a copy of *Fishy Fingers*. The book fell open at an obviously frequently consulted page showing a selection of bones and a diagram of a strange-looking creature. Its resemblance to the animal in the bathroom did not seem marked. Dunnock pointed out features one by one. 'I thought that was an elbow, but it's a knee. I thought these were toes, but they're spines. The mouth is all wrong, it has gills all over the place, and as for the colour…! Not to mention the lack of scales, the way it moves, what it eats. And you wouldn't believe what it can do with its flippers – it turns accepted theory on its head!'

'Whoops,' said the Doctor.

The old man sighed. 'I thought this would be the crowning moment of my career. But instead it has thrown me into self-doubt. I cannot proceed with theories that I know to be false. But I cannot bring myself to admit how wrong I have been. My reputation would never recover!'

'Oh, come on,' said Martha. 'Scientists have to backtrack all the time, surely, as new evidence comes to light. Just publish a new book and everyone'll be bowled over in amazement at your incredible insights.'

Dunnock huffed. 'And what evidence do I produce, young lady? You expect me to explain how I have revised my entire theory with no new fossil discovery, no new analyses…'

'And you can't show them Mervin because he's supposed to have been extinct for a few million years,' Martha realised.

'They would want to put him in a cage! Cut him open! And I…' he smiled shyly. 'I have become quite fond of him. I have provided him with a home, food, female company…'

'You what?' The Doctor sounded incredulous. 'You've found a girlfriend for a millions-of-years-old, extinct half-fish half-mammal? That must have been one heck of an ad you placed in the Lonely Hearts column.'

'Girlfriend-*s*,' the professor corrected him, indicating the other end of the caravan. On a shelf stood a tank and a cage.

'Oh,' said the Doctor blankly. 'His female friends are – a goldfish and a hamster.'

'I didn't know which side of the family he would incline towards,' Dunnock explained.

'Oh,' said the Doctor again, seemingly lost for words. Martha was too.

'And you're definitely not going to tell us who sold him to you?' asked the Doctor when he recovered.

'I can't,' Dunnock said. 'It was dark, my eyes are not good, he wore a plastic mask in the shape of an Iguanodon head…'

'Oh well,' said the Doctor. 'It was worth a try.'

Martha breathed a sigh of relief when they finally exited the caravan, leaving Dunnock preparing a meal of sunflower seeds and ant eggs for his charge. 'That professor smelled a bit like a half-fish, half-mammal,' she commented.

The Doctor grinned. 'Yeah – but we're a bit further on. Only a tiny pixie step on the path of progress it's true, but further on nonetheless.'

'You mean, we know the culprit's a young man.'

He nodded. 'Right. Although given that Dunnock is an extremely old man—'

'And a loony.'

'—and, as you rather perceptively if not elegantly say, a loony, "young" could mean almost anything. But if it's one of the Earthers, as we suspect, it is at least narrowed down to three suspects.'

'Rix, Tommy or Frank.'

They were resetting the coordinates on their pendants as they walked. 'Will "Mervin" be OK?' Martha asked. 'Shouldn't we try to get him – it – back to the museum? I mean, he's living in a sink, looked after by a bloke who's completely barmy.'

'At least the professor doesn't believe in cages,' muttered the Doctor, but he did wrinkle his nose in indecision. Or it might have been due to lingering traces of the caravan's smell. 'I'll think about it,' he said in the end. 'Are you ready? Maybe we'll have more luck at the most recent transaction point.'

She sighed. 'Oh, I guess so. I hope we sort it out this time, though, these people aren't exactly my cup of tea.'

'Mmm, I wouldn't mind a cup of tea,' said the Doctor. 'Maybe the next illegal-extinct-animal purchaser will offer us one.'

But he was destined to be disappointed.

AYE-AYE

Daubentonia madagascariensis

Location: Madagascar

The aye-aye is a nocturnal, forest-dwelling lemur. It has black fur with white around its eyes and nose, and possesses very long middle fingers which it uses to dig out insects to eat. It is approximately 30 centimetres in length, not including the bushy tail which is about one-and-a-half times the length of its body.

Addendum:

Last reported sighting: AD 2042.
Cause of extinction: destruction of habitat.

I-Spyder points value: 500

Creature	Points
Dodo	800
Megatherium	500
Paradise parrot	500
Velociraptor	250
Mountain gorilla	500
Aye-aye	900
Siberian tiger	600
Kakapo	900
Indefatigable Galapagos mouse	1500
Stegosaurus	500
Triceratops	550
Diplodocus	600
Ankylosaurus	650
Dimetrodon	600
Passenger pigeon	100
Thylacine	250
Black rhinoceros	300
Mervin the missing link	23500
Subtotal	33500

SEVEN

In common with the first trip, the Doctor and Martha arrived somewhere staggeringly sumptuous; in common with the second, they found themselves outdoors. In every other respect, this place was as far removed from both of the previous locations as possible. They were under a canopy in a brilliant, sunny garden, amid tinkling fountains and what seemed like a thousand orchids of every colour in the rainbow. A young girl was lying face down on a silk floor cushion and, as she started up at the sound of their arrival, Martha saw that her pretty oriental features were stained with tears.

'Tea is probably not forthcoming,' the Doctor whispered out of the side of his mouth. 'Bother.'

'Who – who are you?' the girl stammered, although the hesitation seemed to have nothing to do with fear, just her sobs.

The Doctor stepped forward and spoke gently. 'I'm the Doctor, and this—'

But he got no further. The girl began to shake her head violently. 'You're too late! Too late! He would not have seen you anyway, not a western doctor – not that it matters now.'

'You mean he's…?' The Doctor was clearly fishing for information.

'He died twenty minutes ago.' She suddenly frowned. 'Why are you here? Why did you not go to the house?'

'We did,' the Doctor lied. 'But we couldn't make anyone hear. So we came looking…' He tailed off, hands spread out to indicate the dilemma of a doctor who could not gain access to the place he had been summoned to. The girl seemed to accept this. In a house of mourning, clearly all could not be expected to run smoothly.

The Doctor went over to the girl, and plonked himself down beside her. After some hesitation, Martha followed. She felt a twinge of guilt – surely they were exploiting this girl's grief? But an investigator couldn't afford such scruples.

'Did he suffer much?' the Doctor asked, sympathy dripping from his voice.

A shiver ran through the girl before she nodded. 'Yes,' she whispered, eventually. 'It was… It was not an easy thing to watch.'

'But I'm sure you did everything you could to help him.'

She smiled then, a smile with not the faintest trace of warmth or happiness. 'I would have dealt with the Devil to save him,' she said.

Martha drew in a deep breath. She believed her. Well, she knew at least one thing that the girl must have done. *One of*

*the reasons they became extinct in the first place – idiots getting it into
their heads that rhino horn could cure all ills.*

Then the cold, inhuman smile vanished, and she was a
sobbing child again, tearful and snotty, a ridiculous figure
amid the beauty and calm of her surroundings. She thrust a
hand into a pocket and rooted blindly for a moment before
pulling out a square of cloth to wipe her face, a strangely
inelegant gesture.

And then Martha jumped. Without quite realising what
was coming out of her mouth, certainly without thinking,
she cried, 'Where did you get that hankie?'

The girl swivelled to look at her, regarding her as though
she were a mad thing. After all, these were the first words
Martha had spoken to her and it was hardly a conventional
address to the recently bereaved. Then she glanced down
at the handkerchief. So did the Doctor, and he had clearly
realised exactly what Martha was thinking.

This was no delicate square of Chinese silk. This was a
great flapping piece of cotton, about a foot square. It was
covered with small print dinosaurs.

The girl looked slightly puzzled herself. 'Oh,' she said
after a second. 'I… found it. Someone must have dropped
it.'

'What "someone"?' said Martha, harshly, because she
knew the answer and didn't want to hear it.

The girl bridled at her tone. 'Just… someone.' She drew
herself up. 'I picked it up. Not that it's any business of
yours.'

'Oh, but it is,' Martha told her, despite the Doctor's
warning hand on her arm. 'If you trade with people like that

you've got to expect a few awkward questions. You know, about handkerchiefs,' she added awkwardly. 'And stuff.'

'The "stuff" being slightly more important,' the Doctor said, rather more gently. 'So perhaps you would tell us who you got the rhino horn from.'

The girl looked terrified. 'He said no one would ever find out!'

'And you trusted him? Oh dear. Oh dear-dear-dear-deary me.' Now the Doctor was a policeman, shaking his head and tutting. 'I think you'd better tell us everything you know about this man.'

'But I never saw him! Truly, I never saw him, never spoke to him face to face, I know nothing about him at all! I just found the handkerchief after the… delivery.'

And, reluctantly, Martha believed her. Not that it mattered. The evidence clearly pointed the way. She reached out and took the sodden square from the girl, holding it up so there could be no mistake in what they were looking at. Both she and the Doctor knew exactly where they'd seen an identical hankie, barely hours before. 'Tommy,' she said sadly.

He nodded. 'I think it's time we got back to the warehouse.'

They shimmered back into existence in the exit-free office. The Doctor had moved through to the main warehouse before Martha had got her head together, but after a few dizzy moments she set off after him. The only person in there was Rix, sitting on an upturned box. There was no sign of his partner.

'Where's Tommy?' the Doctor demanded.

Rix ignored the question. 'So there you are!' he said. 'Sneaking off without a word, we didn't have a clue what was going on!'

'Well, we are private investigators,' Martha told him. 'Emphasis on the "private", you know? Where's Tommy?'

This time he answered. 'He's gone back to round up the others. We did what we could here—' He gestured around him, and Martha tried hard not to look at the corner that she was now sure contained the skinned corpse of the quagga – 'but he thought we needed help. Thought that the others should see what had happened. I stayed on guard.'

'And you just let him go!'

Rix frowned. 'What are you talking about? It's not my business to "let" him do anything. One, he's my boss, and two, why should I want to stop him?'

'Because he's the kidnapping stealing murderer!' Martha blurted out, although the Doctor's exasperated look told her this may not have been the best approach.

The Earther jumped to his feet, then slowly sat down again. 'I don't believe it,' he said dazedly, shaking his head. 'Not Tommy. You must be wrong. Not Tommy.'

'Not Tommy what?' said a cheery voice from behind them. The Doctor and Martha turned round. There was Tommy himself, with the other four Earthers ranged behind him: Vanni and Nadya, Frank and Celia.

Rix stood up again and stumbled towards his partner, arms outstretched. 'Tell me it's not true, Tom, please.'

'Tell you what's not true?'

He pointed at Martha. 'She says it's you that's done all this.'

It looked like Tommy's knees started to give way beneath him; he stumbled backwards and Nadya grabbed his arm to stop him falling. 'Of course I didn't do this,' he said hoarsely, his cheeky grin vanishing completely.

Celia had run over to the still-unconscious rhinoceros and was kneeling beside the great beast, paying no attention to the drama going on elsewhere. 'Oh, the poor thing,' she was saying, stroking its hide. 'We collected him, Frank and I. We collected him. Oh, the poor thing. Frank, look.'

Frank looked half dazed and gave a loud sniff, as if trying to hold back tears. 'Yeah, right, the poor thing,' he echoed.

Rix and Nadya had taken up positions on either side of Tommy. 'I don't believe for a second that Tommy had anything to do with the disappearances,' said Nadya, addressing Martha. 'Tell me what proof you have.'

Slowly, reluctantly, Martha drew the dinosaur-print handkerchief from her pocket and held it up. 'This was found at the scene of the crime.'

There was a silence. A puzzled silence.

Then Vanni said, 'I don't understand. What does that prove?'

Martha frowned, glancing down at the handkerchief then back at the group in front of her. 'It's Tommy's,' she said. 'We saw him use an identical one earlier. And you have to admit it's fairly distinctive.'

But even Tommy himself seemed to have relaxed. 'But we all have those!' he cried. 'They come from the museum gift shop! Eve gave us all one for Christmas.'

'Cheapskate that she is,' muttered Nadya.

'And I still have mine!' Tommy continued. 'You saw it!'

Triumphantly, he pulled the cotton square from his pocket.

Martha relaxed too. Tommy wasn't the criminal! She had liked him; she was glad. She turned to the Doctor, smiling. 'Not Tommy!' she said.

'But someone else…' he pointed out. He looked at Rix, at Nadya, at Vanni, at Frank. He looked at Celia, still nursing the rhino, which seemed to be beginning to stir under her ministrations.

'Oh yes,' said Martha. 'That's true. Er, we could ask them all to turn out their pockets? You know, for hankies?'

'Oh, I don't think there's any need for that,' said the Doctor. 'I think it's fairly obvious who's missing one, don't you? Only a person who had mislaid their hankie earlier in the day would sniff as much as you, Frank!' He threw out an arm dramatically, pointing an accusatory finger at the stocky Earther.

Who drew a gun out of his pocket.

'I don't believe it! I was right!' said the Doctor, backing away. 'Frank, Frankie, Frankie-boy, you could have at least tried to bluff it out. Tell the truth, it was a bit of a wild guess on my part. The absence of a hankie isn't your actual cast-iron proof at all, more sort of fluffy, marshmallow, knock-it-down-with-a-feather proof.'

'I never even took my handkerchief out of the wrapping,' put in Vanni, helpfully. 'Silly cheap thing.'

'Shut up!' shouted Frank, waving the gun first this way then that. 'Look, I didn't want anyone to get hurt.'

'Except the animals!' cried Martha, regretting it almost at once as the gun veered decisively towards her.

Frank shrugged. 'Yeah, right, animals. All I ever hear

about is animals, animals, animals. What about people, huh? You can do a lot of good with a few million, but what's the use of some stupid zebra in a cage? No bloomin' use at all, that's what.'

'So you were planning to use your ill-gotten gains to do good for humanity?' asked the Doctor, interestedly.

'Duh, yeah, right. I was planning to spend it on myself, of course,' Frank admitted. 'Just making a point. And, bit of a cliché and all that, but now you know too much and I'm gonna have to silence you.' He raised the gun. It was now aimed straight at the Doctor.

'Ah,' said the Doctor. 'Mind you, talking about making a point…'

Frank's finger tightened on the trigger.

And the shot blasted into the ceiling, as he went flying backwards over the charging rhino's nose.

Nadya grabbed the gun. Rix and Tommy grabbed the dazed Frank, Tommy yanking off his pendant to prevent any escape attempts. Celia, one hand on her own pendant, was running after the rhinoceros; a second later, girl and beast both vanished.

The Doctor stood there with a big grin on his face, as a trickle of falling plaster dust began to sprinkle his hair.

'"Making a point"?' said Martha critically.

'Good, wasn't it?' The Doctor was still grinning.

'But it doesn't work.'

'Doesn't work?'

'The pun doesn't work! You saw that the rhino was getting up, and you were making a pun about it butting Frank with its horn. Except it doesn't have a horn any more.'

'So it doesn't,' said the Doctor. 'That was a bit *pointless*, then.'

Martha groaned.

We all zapped back to the museum. The first thing I saw was another empty cage, about the right size for a gorilla or something, and I panicked that we'd been too late to save some other poor creature – but Tommy said it was a box that hadn't been filled yet; obviously some new arrival was expected. By the time we turned up, the rhino was already back in its place, and I couldn't help but think that it deserved a better reward for saving all our lives than being frozen for all eternity. The Doctor's views were starting to rub off on me.

Celia was sat on the floor outside the rhino's box with her elbows on her knees. She didn't seem anywhere near as stuck up now as my first impression of her; I guess finding out your partner is actually a baddie tends to knock you for six a bit.

'We collected it together, Frank and I,' she said. 'It was in a wildlife reserve in Kenya, and we arrived just in time to stop a poacher from shooting it.'

'What was a poacher doing in a wildlife reserve?' I asked, shocked.

She laughed humourlessly. 'Reserves are like sweet shops to poachers. Everything gathered together in one place for them.' Her eyes glazed over and I guess she was back in time. 'He nearly shot me too. I was so angry, I went for him instead of attending to the rhinoceros. If Frank hadn't knocked his gun aside…'

It looked like she was about to cry. I hastily suggested a cup of tea, and she nodded gratefully, at which point I realised I had no idea how to procure such a thing.

'Let's go to the cafeteria,' said Vanni, and I smiled at her gratefully.

I wondered if the Doctor would come along too – after all, he had been hankering after a cuppa earlier – but he shook his head. 'You go,' he said. 'I'll go along with the others, see Eve, sort this all out. See you in a bit.'

So Frank was led off, a little procession, and then me, Vanni and Celia went the other way.

EASTERN BLACK RHINOCEROS

Diceros bicornis michaeli

Location: Eastern Africa

The leathery skin of this aggressive herbivore is not black but grey in colour. It has two curving horns on its snout, the longer front one measuring around half to one metre. These are made of tough hair. The rhinoceros has three hooves on each foot. Its upper lip curves over the lower one.

Addendum:

Last reported sighting: AD 2051.
Cause of extinction: poaching for their horns and for the bush meat trade.

I-Spyder points value: 300

Creature	Points
Dodo	800
Megatherium	500
Paradise parrot	500
Velociraptor	250
Mountain gorilla	500
Aye-aye	900
Siberian tiger	600
Kakapo	900
Indefatigable Galapagos mouse	1500
Stegosaurus	500
Triceratops	550
Diplodocus	600
Ankylosaurus	650
Dimetrodon	600
Passenger pigeon	100
Thylacine	250
Black rhinoceros	300
Mervin the missing link	23500
Subtotal	33500

EIGHT

The cafeteria wasn't manned, instead being full of vending machines; I guess that's why it was still open at this time of night. Vanni got us three cups of tea and three doughnuts. There was something pretty reassuring about finding out they still have doughnuts in the future. Mine had raspberry jam in the middle.

I won't go into what was said, all the recriminations and disbelief interspersed with a bit of weeping here and there. The sort of thing you get when someone's just split up with their boyfriend, only a bit worse. I expect you can imagine. I could understand her feelings – after all, I can't think how I'd feel if I discovered the Doctor had been going around chopping up pet dogs or something. But still, it got a bit wearing after a bit – I mean, this girl wasn't even a friend of mine. But what can you do? I started to hope the Doctor would reappear and whisk me back to the TARDIS – and when you begin to wish you're facing monsters instead, you know it's getting bad. But no Doctor.

Anyway, I guess Vanni was feeling it too, cos after a while she started to yawn. Celia got all apologetic after that; well, it turns out Vanni should have been off-shift hours ago; she was only still up because of all that had been going on. It was Frank and Celia who were supposed to be the Earthers on duty at the moment, and realising that made Celia go all sobby again.

And then Celia's pendant started to beep. 'Oh no!' she cried, staring at us both, horrified. 'What do I do?' Turns out this was her cue for action, but of course she didn't have anyone to take action with any more.

'Ask Eve,' Vanni said, and Celia flicked a switch on the back of her pendant, one that I hadn't noticed before.

'Eve?' she said. 'What do I do? I can't do it on my own!'

Eve's voice crackled out of the tiny device. 'Celia. One moment, please.' There was a pause, then: 'The Doctor suggests that Martha could accompany you for now. He and I are busy, currently. It will give her something to do.'

Well, I won't deny I resented that just a little bit. It was so like the Doctor, handing out jobs for you to do while he was off doing goodness-knows-what elsewhere, and I'd really had about as much as I could take of Celia for one night – but, there again, I was feeling a bit fascinated about exactly what the Earthers did, and it might take her mind off Frank's betrayal for a bit. So I just shrugged and said, 'OK.'

'Good,' said Eve's voice. 'I'll programme you in. Be ready, time is precious.' So we sat there, tense and alert, for what seemed like far too long. I was trying in vain to think of something to say, when – thank goodness – my pendant started beeping, just like Celia's.

'Good luck,' said Vanni, yawning again and standing up. I think she was pretty relieved too. As she headed off to her bed, I waved goodnight, then, watching Celia's hand rising to do the same, pressed the pendant's blue button.

And would you believe, I was never for a second suspicious that the Doctor had been such a long time, or that I hadn't heard his voice in the background over the pendant intercom or anything.

Didn't cross my mind for a moment.

I'm really not much of a detective, am I?

'Hello,' said the Doctor, bounding into Eve's office ahead of the others, 'solved your mystery for you. Good, eh?'

She looked up, and there was something in her eyes, something close to excitement. Nervousness and anticipation were there too. 'Good,' she said, but didn't seem to be focusing on the matter at hand, didn't even ask what the solution was. Even when Tommy, Rix and Nadya led in the sullen Frank, her attention was clearly elsewhere.

Frank was given short shrift. No attempts at justification were allowed, no defence, no condemnations of meddling kids. The security guards were summoned at once, and he was led off to a cell to await a full legal investigation.

Eve dismissed the remaining three Earthers. 'None of you are on shift,' she said. 'Better get some rest while you can.' Nodding their thanks, they all retired.

That left just the Doctor.

'Thank you,' Eve said at last.

He shrugged his shoulders. 'I won't say "my pleasure",' he told her. 'Just because I disliked what Frank was doing more than I dislike what you are doing, doesn't mean you're suddenly my favourite person in the universe. In some ways he was almost more admirable: at least he wasn't trying to pretend he has some great altruistic purpose.'

'And I am pretending?'

'Well, I'd call this place pretty selfish overall. You're hardly doing it for the animals; you're just a glorified stamp collector.' He threw up his arms and spun round, taking in the dull functionality of the office. 'There's no passion here!'

Eve half-rose from her seat, then sank back down again. 'I care!' she almost spat at him. 'This place is everything to me!'

The Doctor perched himself on the edge of her desk. 'I believe you,' he said. 'Like I believe getting a British Guiana One Cent Magenta or a Tre Skilling Banco Yellow would mean everything to the stamp collector.' He leant forward and spoke confidentially. 'You remember Martha? Course you do, only met her a few hours ago. Well, she and I had a little disagreement over the merits of zoos back on her home planet. And, being exceptionally intelligent and open-minded as I am, I can see both sides of the argument. Lot of people thinking they're doing a lot of good. Education, conservation, breeding, a bunch of Noahs in a metaphorical flood. And the thing is, if you were doing something like that here, I might be able to sympathise a bit more. Rescuing two of every animal. Breeding. Even cloning. But you're not.'

This time Eve did leave her seat. 'Come with me,' she said, walking rapidly to the door.

The Doctor, never knowingly nonplussed, followed her.

He wasn't all that surprised to find that they ended up in the Earth section again. 'You know,' he remarked, 'I'm always getting teased about Earth. Keep ending up there, whether I mean to or not. Seems like even when I avoid the planet itself, I can't escape it.' He leaned over to examine a minuscule box containing a bright-green beetle.

Eve kept on walking. 'Have you ever had a dream?' she said.

The Doctor, catching up, waved an airy hand around. 'Well, there's this one where I'm being chased by a Slitheen on a rocking horse,' he said, 'but to be honest I don't sleep very much so it's no big deal. Or are you asking if I have visions of a universe united in peace and harmony?'

'My dream was destroyed,' Eve told him, ignoring his answer. 'Destroyed a long time ago. Or... maybe not so long after all. It's hard to say, even for me. My life's work could never be complete. Or so I thought.'

'That elusive One Cent Magenta?' the Doctor asked, interested.

'If you like to put it like that. The one planet that eluded me. Destroyed utterly, never to be represented here. The only one, ever.'

'Well, them's the breaks,' the Doctor said. 'You can hardly expect extinctions to happen at your convenience.' They had just reached the Black Rhinoceros, and he was momentarily distracted. He took out his sonic screwdriver from his pocket, an automatic response to seeing something trapped – then tossed it from hand to hand, not quite sure what to do. 'Half the human race have the problem that they see animals as objects. The other half have the problem that they anthropomorphise them. Can't blame those ones so much, though. I look at this animal, and I think "what a noble beast". Especially with it saving our lives and all that. And yet it's hardly as if it subscribes to the code of the Knights Templar, or was acting out of some virtuous desire to rescue a damsel in distress. I'm talking about Martha,' he pointed out hurriedly. 'This Time Lord's neither a damsel nor distressed.'

There was a sudden silence.

'Time Lord,' said Eve, huskily, the words almost catching in her throat.

The Doctor stood absolutely still, not looking at her, staring unseeingly at the frozen rhino.

'The last Time Lord.'

The Doctor still said nothing.

'The only survivor. The only specimen.'

He moved then, spinning round, eyes blazing with anger and hurt. No fear though, even knowing, as he couldn't help knowing then, what was in her mind. 'The One Cent Magenta,' he snarled.

And she took him completely unawares.

He'd expected verbal sparring. She was alone, she was unarmed, she was a short woman and he was a tall man. He held all the cards.

But she was a collector, and she was a fanatic, and he didn't expect what happened next.

Eve ran at him, her head down. She butted him right in the middle of his stomach, and, surprised, he staggered backwards. Couldn't stop himself. Spiralling his arms to try to regain his balance, sonic screwdriver dropping to the floor, he found himself propelled into an empty perspex box. A vague memory surfaced through the whirling thoughts in his head: Martha worrying that another creature had been stolen and Tommy telling her no, this box must have been prepared for a new specimen.

And then Eve was throwing herself at the small keypad at the top of the cage, and in that second everything ended for the Doctor.

Eve sank down on the carpeted walkway, staring up at her latest acquisition. Now it was all over, any trace there may have been of emotion had vanished, and, although her first words were 'I'm sorry', there was no hint of regret; they were just standard words, a formula to introduce the point she was making. 'I'm sorry,' she said, addressing the petrified Time Lord in front of her. 'I know you're not in the right place, which is undignified, but, as I'm sure you will understand, there is no section for your planet, as yet. I will have one constructed, but at the moment I'm afraid you'll have to remain here. Seems like even when you avoid the planet Earth, you can't escape it,' she paraphrased.

She sat there for a long time, just looking. Some of the collection agents had had problems in the past when expected to gather higher-order specimens: sentient, self-aware, intelligent. Eve had no such problem. Their preservation was for the greater good. If she had been more empathic, Eve might even have made the argument that letting something live out its life knowing it was the only one of its kind was a far crueller fate. But her only thoughts were for the Collection.

Something would have to be done about the display: the shocked, angry, disbelieving look on the Doctor's face was just not appropriate, nor was his gravity-defying pose, falling backwards with arms raised. It might worry some of the younger visitors. She would conceal the exhibit for now. Oh, and there was the Doctor's friend to be considered, too, of course. She would probably have some absurd emotional reaction to the situation: she would have to be got out of the way. As a human, she had no intrinsic value, there were still billions of them around…

It might have been then that an idea started to form in Eve's mind.

But her immediate problem was Martha. And just then a sound started up, an alert, relating to the Earth section. Another species on the brink of extinction; just another day at the office for MOTLO. Then there was a beep, an attempt at communication. 'Eve?' came Celia's voice, distressed. 'What do I do? I can't do it on my own!'

'Celia. One moment, please.' Of course, Celia was on duty – although her partner was currently unavailable, thanks to the Doctor. But in the short term… the phrase 'killing two birds with one stone' fitted the case perfectly, ironic indeed for a venture dedicated to saving life. Eve looked at the frozen figure in front of her. 'The Doctor suggests that Martha could accompany you for now. He and I are busy, currently. It will give her something to do.' She didn't smile knowingly; she didn't give an evil laugh. It was a lie to achieve a purpose – it gave her no pleasure nor caused her any distress.

There was a moment's pause, then a background voice, that of Martha, could be heard saying 'OK.'

'Good,' Eve said. 'I'll programme you in. Be ready, time is precious.'

She pushed herself up from the floor, regaining her feet in one swift, perfectly balanced movement, then walked briskly back to the door that would transport her to her office. It wasn't long before she was sat in front of the computer and enabling Martha's travel pendant to receive the same alert transmissions and coordinates as Celia's.

Seconds later, a little window popped up on her screen to inform her that the two women had left the museum, hot on the trail.

But of course the problem of Martha had not been resolved, just postponed.

TASMANIAN TIGER

Thylacinus cynocephalus

Location: Australasia

The doglike Tasmanian tiger, also known as the Thylacine, is a carnivorous, predatory marsupial. It has a smooth brown coat with black or darker brown stripes on its rear and is approximately 160 centimetres in length, with about a third of that being its tail. The male is generally larger than the female.

Addendum:

Last reported sighting: AD 1936.
Cause of extinction: hunting by man (several bounties were placed on the animals' heads during the 19th and early 20th centuries); disease.

I-Spyder points value: 300

Creature	Points
Dodo	800
Megatherium	500
Paradise parrot	500
Velociraptor	250
Mountain gorilla	500
Aye-aye	900
Siberian tiger	600
Kakapo	900
Indefatigable Galapagos mouse	1500
Stegosaurus	500
Triceratops	550
Diplodocus	600
Ankylosaurus	650
Dimetrodon	600
Passenger pigeon	100
Thylacine	250
Black rhinoceros	300
Mervin the missing link	23500
Subtotal	33500

NINE

There was a time, once, when I was caged.

I wanted to wander, and They said: No. But I needed – I need – to wander, and so it hurt. It really hurt.

They said: But at least you're safe there. No danger. Not like in your wandering days.

No danger, perhaps. But no life, either.

They said: Really, it's for your own good.

But who were They to decide? They'd never lived as I had, never traversed the wide open spaces, felt the adrenalin of the chase, seen the beauty – the incomparable, indescribable beauty of my natural habitat.

For my own good, indeed!

See me pacing the tiny space, trapped. I was going out of my mind! They watched me. They used me. They said: You can help the people around you.

So I did, because I had no choice. The people around me treated me like a resource, not understanding that their every desire tightened the chains that bound me.

But of course They didn't care.

Now They're all gone. There's only me left. I'm free, now.

I'm the last of my kind, and I miss Them. You'd think I'd forgive Them for what they did, so long ago. But I can't. Some things are unforgivable.

I was a Time Lord in exile.

Or was I an animal in a zoo?

Martha blinked, her pupils contracting suddenly after the transition from the dim artificial light of the MOTLO canteen to brilliant sunshine. If her eardrums had been able to contract too they would have done; the increase in the ambient sound was even greater. Traders hawked their wares at top volume, old women haggled over prices, young men shouted to each other across the market place, but above it all were the animal noises: howlings, growlings, screeches and shrieks, the clucking of chickens and quacking of ducks.

She took in a lungful of the heady, spicy atmosphere. Even without the evidence of her eyes, she would have known she was in the Orient again, but nothing could contrast more with the serenity of the garden she had visited earlier. Bustle was the order of the day. Luckily this meant that everyone was far too busy with their own business to notice two western-looking women appearing abruptly in a side street.

Celia sniffed. 'Frank used to love markets,' she said.

'Yeah, he was probably comparing prices,' said Martha, her sympathy almost entirely exhausted by now. Then she did a mental double take. 'Hang on, you mean you come to places like this a lot? I've heard of people trading in endangered animals, but they're not going to do it in the open like this, are they?'

'Don't be naive,' said Celia. 'It happens all the time. Or else they just don't know or don't care.' She held up her pendant, using it like a compass, then pointed towards a stall with crates stacked in front of it. 'That's where we want to be.'

They threaded their way through the crowd, passing rows of squawking chickens suspended from ropes by their feet, hearing the barking of caged dogs that Martha couldn't bear to look at. London's food markets, with their organic veg and local cheeses and men yelling about 'free pahndsa strawbries fra pahnd', seemed worlds away.

The crates Celia had indicated turned out to contain heaped piles of turtles. A few curious chelonian heads swung up to look as she plunged her hands in and began to sort through the stacks of shells. The stallholder beamed across at the two women. 'Yes, yes, take your time, all are very good,' he said.

Finally Celia located her prize, and pointed out a turtle that Martha would have been hard-pressed to distinguish from all the others if it hadn't been for the three black stripes on its back. She couldn't really get her head around it: this little brown and green creature – with its surprisingly cute face for a reptile – was the only one of its kind on Earth. That was hard to deal with. This was it, journey's end for an entire species. What made it really difficult, though, was the banality of it all. People going about their ordinary, everyday business and suddenly whoops, no more turtles, and did any of them give a monkey's? Didn't seem like it. Without them, some diner would have tucked into his turtle soup, not caring that he would be the last person in the universe ever to be near even the remains of a unique creature.

A thought struck her. 'You got the call to come here, what, minutes ago?'

Celia nodded.

'And you get the call when the little light goes on in Eve's office, that means there's only one animal left.'

Another nod.

'But then… a few minutes ago, there must have been another one. Another turtle. There must have been two turtles, and then something happened to one of them, and now this is the only one left.'

'That's right.'

Martha screwed up her forehead. 'But… but… that means that if we'd known about it just a little bit earlier, we could have saved that other turtle too. It might have been, you know, a boy turtle. If this one's a girl turtle. Or the other way around. You could have taken them both back, and they'd have had little baby turtles, and the baby turtles would have had baby turtles, and yes, OK, we're talking a bit of inbreeding here, but the species would have been saved. All for the sake of a minute or two!'

'It'd hardly be the Museum of the Last Ones, then,' Celia pointed out. 'It would be the Museum of the Last Two, for a while, until they start breeding and then who knows?'

Martha nodded hard. 'But that's the point!'

The other girl looked exasperated. 'The last one is what we're told about, so the last one is what we get. Don't ask me how the technology works, maybe it can only pick up the trace when there's one left.'

Martha held her hands to her head, trying to think of a way of articulating the thoughts swimming around in it. 'But surely, sometimes you're not gonna make it in time.' She remembered a story the Doctor had told her earlier in the day. 'Like – the Great Auk, right? There was only one pair left in the whole world, and their egg. Then this collector sends a couple of blokes to get him a skin, and they club the birds to death and trample on their egg.' She stopped for a second, feeling slightly sick. 'All dead in moments, not much time for you to swoop in and carry off the last one to its new space home. And he said he didn't see one listed in the museum. But if you'd gone years earlier, picked up a few when they were all swimming around in the sea, taken them somewhere safe… It wouldn't have to be a museum at all any more.' She unconsciously echoed the Doctor's earlier thoughts. 'It'd be a sort of Noah's Ark! Wouldn't that be better?'

Celia narrowed her eyes. 'Look, it's Eve's museum, and it's her decision. At least we're doing something. I mean, this is your planet, isn't it? I've not noticed you dashing around saving two of every kind.'

Martha was about to respond – not that she was entirely sure what she was going to say – when she noticed that the stallholder, who had fished out the turtle and was holding it up by a leg, had picked up a cleaver in his other hand. The little creature was struggling, fighting against gravity and the man's grasp to try to draw its limbs and head into the safety of its shell. 'No!' she yelped. 'Don't kill it!' She grabbed the animal from the man and he shrugged, unconcerned.

The turtle, placid again, twisted its stripy head round and regarded Martha calmly, not knowing the deadly fate from which it had been saved; not knowing the just-as-final fate for which it was now destined.

Celia handed over a small piece of plastic, the size and shape of a credit card but with a tiny display screen on the front. The trader pushed it into a reader on his stall and an amount flashed green on the screen as the transaction went through.

Martha was feeling restless and dissatisfied. She hadn't wanted to do this, certainly hadn't wanted to hang around with Celia, but she'd assumed that there was a sort of nobility in the work, a passion that inspired the collection agents. She expected them to be Indiana Jones types, facing down big-game hunters and ruthless rainforest destroyers, engaged in battles to the death to rescue animals small and furry or tall and proud. While she'd sympathised with the Doctor's anti-MOTLO stance, she had felt admiration for the Earthers, risking their lives to preserve these precious creatures – and to save the human race from the catastrophic consequences of their actions.

Instead… they'd popped down to Earth, bought the Last One for a few *dong* and would be back in time for breakfast.

The two women weren't looking at each other as they walked back towards the alleyway, but if either one had turned she would have seen a mirror image of her own mulish expression on the other's face. And each was concentrating so hard on ignoring the other that they failed at first to notice that something was happening to their pendants. But it was soon impossible to ignore. 'Hey!'

Martha held hers up. 'It's glowing! Why's it doing that?' she asked the air in front of her.

But realisation had swept away Celia's mood. She looked at Martha's pendant, then her own. 'It's like an alarm,' she said, puzzled and anxious. 'It's telling us to get a move on…'

'What, to get back to the museum?'

'No! To rescue the Last One…'

Martha looked down at the little turtle. 'But we have.'

Celia looked at the turtle too. Then she bent down to look at it more closely. Then she straightened up, took a deep breath and closed her eyes. Then she opened them, looked at the turtle again and shouted: 'Where are the stripes? This isn't the right turtle!'

'What?'

'We were sent to collect a Three-Striped Box Turtle, so named because it has three stripes on its back. This has no stripes on its back. It has a yellow and black head. This has got red stripes on its head! You got the wrong one!'

'Me?!' said Martha indignantly. 'I just took the one the stallholder handed me!'

But Celia wasn't listening any more, she'd already set off at a run. Martha followed her but, by the time she reached the stall, Celia was already yelling at the turtle seller in a voice so high-pitched it was very unlikely he could understand a word she said.

'You sold us the wrong turtle,' Martha clarified, seeing the man's look of incomprehension. 'Let me talk to him,' she told the other girl. 'You find the right one.'

Celia dived into the crate, as Martha turned back to the

salesman – who didn't seem particularly concerned. 'That is a good turtle,' he said, pointing at the one in Martha's hands. 'You will get no better turtle.'

'Yes, but it's not the one we picked out,' she told him. 'And we wanted that one particularly.'

He shrugged. 'That is a good turtle,' he said again. 'You will get no better turtle.'

'Yes,' she said again, trying to remain patient, 'but it's not the one we picked out.'

Celia was getting more frantic by the second. Suddenly she threw her hands into the air. 'It's not here!' she cried.

'Are you sure?' Martha asked. Celia looked ready to explode again, so she backed down. 'All right, all right, you're sure.' She asked the stallholder: 'Have you sold any turtles since we were here?'

'I sell many turtles,' he told her proudly. 'They are all good turtles. You will get no better turtles.'

'Yes, but…' She took a deep breath. 'There was a turtle. We wanted the turtle. Now it's gone. Please could you tell us what happened to it. Did you sell it to someone else?'

'I sell many turtles,' he said again, causing Martha's blood pressure to rise. 'You expect me to remember all of them?'

'Well, seeing as we'd only been gone about four minutes, yeah, I'd expect you to remember this one. Or did it become turtle central after we left, with everyone in the market suddenly descending on you demanding turtles?'

He gave in. 'Old lady,' he said. 'White hair, pink bag. Went that way.' As they raced off in the direction indicated, he shouted after them, 'But that is a good turtle!'

'Pink bag, pink bag,' muttered Martha as she ran. The

pendant was glowing brighter. They dashed this way and that as traces of pink were spotted, only to find themselves chasing a cerise scarf or a crimson sleeve.

'There!' gasped Celia at last, and they charged towards a little white-haired, pink-bag-toting old lady. 'Excuse me,' she panted, 'but I think you may have our turtle.'

The old woman looked affronted. 'You say I have stolen a turtle?'

'No, no.' Martha hastened to smooth things over. 'You see, we bought a turtle. But the stallholder gave it to you by mistake. We just want our turtle back.'

The woman pointed at the turtle in Martha's hand. 'You have a turtle.'

'Yes, but…' This was getting tedious. 'It's the wrong turtle. That's our one.' She pointed to the pink bag.

'Now it is my one. I am going to make soup. I cut off head, cut off legs, chop up nice, make soup.'

'But it's a very rare turtle!' Martha told her.

She shrugged. 'Still taste nice.'

'Really, really rare. Look, we'll give you money for it. Lots of money.'

'And you have lots of money, do you?' Celia hissed under her breath.

'You've got that card thing!' Martha waited, palm outstretched, until Celia handed it over, then waved it at the old woman. 'Lots of money!'

'Cash,' she stated firmly. 'How can I take that?'

Martha was ready to tear her hair out. 'But we don't have any cash!'

'Then you do not get my turtle!'

Martha turned to Celia and raised her hands in defeat.

The other girl held out her own hand, and Martha offered the credit card back – but Celia took her by surprise by grabbing the turtle, too. She proffered it to the old woman, a pleading look in her eyes. 'Please,' she said, and something must have touched a nerve. The woman nodded, and reached in her bag. Seconds later, Celia was holding a little reptile with three black stripes on the back of its shell, and Martha's turtle was tucked inside the pink straw bag.

Celia snapped into Earther mode, using the pendant to freeze the small creature into immobility, but Martha was staring after the departing woman in dismay. 'But… she'll kill that turtle. Eat it.'

'Yes, she will,' said Celia. 'That's what happens. Did you think we were at a pet store?'

'But we can't just let her go and cut its head off.'

Celia's face hardened. 'There's a whole crate of turtles back there. They're all going to be killed. You want to rescue them all, take them back to the wild? They'll be caught again by some peasant wanting the money, and be back at the market tomorrow. And you know what? You'd have just upped the demand for turtles, and they'd catch a load extra to replace them.'

'But…' Martha knew Celia was telling the truth – but she knew, too, that she didn't want to live her life like that. 'Not being able to do everything doesn't mean you shouldn't do anything,' she said. 'You just have to do as much as you can. Save one turtle here. Save one person there. I know I can't heal everyone in the world, but that's not going to stop me being a doctor.'

There was a pause, during which Martha thought 'oops' and Celia's eyes widened. 'I thought you were supposed to be some sort of detective.'

'I'm undercover?' suggested Martha hopefully.

'A doctor working undercover as a detective?'

'Um… Look, that doesn't matter right now; I'm going after the other turtle.' Martha turned her back on Celia, looking round for the old woman. But while they'd been arguing, she'd disappeared.

Martha was ready to start searching – but Celia grabbed hold of the pendant round her neck, nearly strangling her. 'I think you've got some explaining to do to Eve,' she said, pressing the blue button…

They both disappeared.

And so the other turtle died.

CHINESE THREE-STRIPED BOX TURTLE

Cuora trifasciata

Location: China, Vietnam

This turtle can easily be recognised by the three black stripes on its brown carapace. It also has a black stripe on its green or yellow head.

Addendum:

Last reported sighting: AD 2062.
Cause of extinction: hunting by man for meat and medicine trade.

I-Spyder points value: 700

Creature	Points
Dodo	800
Megatherium	500
Paradise parrot	500
Velociraptor	250
Mountain gorilla	500
Aye-aye	900
Siberian tiger	600
Kakapo	900
Indefatigable Galapagos mouse	1500
Stegosaurus	500
Triceratops	550
Diplodocus	600
Ankylosaurus	650
Dimetrodon	600
Passenger pigeon	100
Thylacine	250
Black rhinoceros	300
Mervin the missing link	23500
Tau duck	5
Dong tao chicken	4
Red-eared slider	40
Chinese three-striped box turtle	350
Subtotal	33899

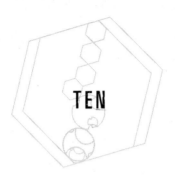

TEN

Celia and Martha materialised in the Earth section, but in an area unfamiliar to Martha. The museum's arrangements seemed haphazard to her: reptiles mingling with mammals; fish next to birds; creatures from the Cretaceous period side by side with animals that had still been alive in her day. Here, the turtle's new home was adjacent to a box containing a dragonfly nearly a metre across, with a terrifying-looking bird towering behind, its head the size of a horse and its beak hooked and vicious. According to a small sign it was a phorusrhacos, and Martha made up her mind then and there to look it up in the *I-Spyder* guide as soon as possible, so she could find out exactly when and where it walked the Earth and ask the Doctor never, ever to take her there.

But she didn't have time to spare for that sort of thing now. Celia had taken a brief second to check that the turtle was properly in place, and had then flicked the switch on the back of her pendant and called Eve.

Martha wasn't really worried. After all, she hadn't

exactly committed a crime, and anyway, the Doctor would soon straighten everything out. So she was a bit surprised when, after Celia had explained to Eve that Martha was an impostor, Eve ordered security guards to arrest her and lock her up.

'Hey! I want to talk to the Doctor!' Martha called.

But Eve's voice came back over the tiny, tinny speaker: 'The Doctor is indisposed.' Now what did *that* mean? One thing Martha did know, she wasn't going to meekly submit to being stuck in prison for however many months.

Time had been passing at the museum while they were gone, and it was now open for business. Martha thought this was a good thing, because Celia probably wouldn't expect her to make a fuss in front of all the visitors – and she certainly wouldn't expect her to clobber the newly arrived security guard and make a run for it.

But that's just what Martha did.

I ran. I've always been a good runner, anyway, and I've had quite a lot of practice since meeting the Doctor, so, even though Celia and the guards know this place better than me, I still managed to evade them. Hurrah for me! Ducking and dodging and hiding are also things I've got better at recently.

Mind you, I didn't really know what to do after I'd finished the running and the hiding et cetera. Museum big as a planet and all that, it doesn't really narrow down your options. I still had the pendant, yes, but as I only knew the coordinates for the places I'd already been to, like the doorless warehouse and the Vietnamese market – none of which contained the

Doctor – that was very much a last resort. The only thing I could think of was to try to make my way back to the TARDIS, although what I would do when I got there I didn't have a clue, unless the Doctor was leaning out of the door waving at me – unlikely, but I cherished a hope anyway. Ms Optimist, that's me.

The TARDIS was still in the Earth section, as far as I knew, and the great thing about being on the run in a museum open to the public is that everywhere is signposted. So, despite the size of the place, all I had to do was pick up a guidebook and follow the directions to the dodo. And as the clock had ticked round to opening time, it meant that (a) I didn't have to worry about movement sensors or anything, and (b) there were members of the general public around to act as camouflage. I say general public; there was as much variety in them as in the exhibits: lizard-men and one-eyed green creatures with dodgy haircuts and some jelly-like blobs that didn't seem to have any eyes, but must have been able to see the exhibits somehow as they were commenting loudly on them.

It was also reassuring to know that there weren't CCTV cameras hidden around, so unless I actually ran into a guard or one of the Earthers I'd met earlier, I was pretty much invisible. Actually, a guard did pass me at one point, looking suspicious, but I cunningly grabbed a nearby small lizard-child and started to lecture it on the Steller's sea cow (poor confused child, it now thinks that Earth is full of Sea Farms, containing Sea Pigs, Sea Chickens and Sea Sheep giving Sea Wool for Sea Sweaters), and that seemed to put him off the scent.

But it did make me think a bit. There's me joking, but I'm actually seeing a Steller's sea cow, something wiped out in the eighteenth century, according to the *I-Spyder* book. I'm seeing all these things that no one else of my time will ever see. Funny how quickly you take things for granted, going 'oh, there's a passenger pigeon, there's a Tasmanian tiger, there's a woolly mammoth.' I suppose it's hard to put them in context. I mean, a lot of the things here seem to be, you know, everyday sorts of frogs, or birds, or mice. Like the turtle – if I'd stumbled across one on Earth, I wouldn't have had a clue they were unique, otherwise extinct creatures – after all, there are hundreds of thousands of frogs and birds and mice on Earth and I'd only recognise the tiniest number of them. It takes things like the dodo to bring it home to you, things you know you couldn't possibly see in the normal run of things.

I'm seeing things that no one else of my time will ever see, visiting places that no one else of my time will ever visit, and I'm treating it like a school trip. The trouble is, I'm always so busy running away from things or hiding from things or looking for clues that I don't have time for anything else. Speaking of which…

I was making my way through the displays, getting to the bit that was becoming quite familiar: the lair of the Black Rhinoceros. And that's when I saw it. Lying on the ground.

The sonic screwdriver.

Now, you might say I've not known the Doctor for very long. You might say that, therefore, I don't know him that well. Well, yeah, maybe, in some ways; I certainly wouldn't feel able to take him as my specialist subject on *Mastermind*, for example – although even after such a short acquaintance I bet I'd score better marks than most people in the universe. So, despite all that, I knew one thing for sure, and that's that he wouldn't just leave his sonic screwdriver lying around. The Doctor forgetting his sonic screwdriver would be like Jordan popping out without her lip gloss.

I looked down at the sonic screwdriver. I bent down and picked up the sonic screwdriver. Then as I stood up I saw something new. A covered box.

When I thought about it for a second, I realised there had been a box there before, empty, when we came back after the rhino rescue affair. But it hadn't been covered.

The box, so far as I could tell, was maybe a couple of feet taller than me, and an arm span wide. Not only was it covered, but it was roped off. Now, once upon a time, I would have respected a boundary like that. I'm quite happy to follow a 'Keep off the grass' sign or a 'No entry'; I mean, I just assume there's a good reason for it. But right now? Ha, no puny length of nylon cord was going to keep me away, and damn the consequences!

So I stepped over the rope (in a rather ungainly fashion it must be admitted, having slightly underestimated the necessary leg-raising height), and I took hold of the cover with both hands, and I yanked as hard as I could.

I think that, somehow, I'd known what I was going to find. There was a sort of dull shock, a moment of losing all my breath, but I must have been subconsciously prepared or I couldn't have assimilated it so quickly, couldn't have pulled myself together as well as I did.

I don't really need to tell you what I saw, do I?

Oh, all right, if you want it spelled out – there, in the box – in the *cage* – was the Doctor.

He'd obviously been taken unawares, his pose and expression showed that.

And his expression showed something else too.

It was frozen, of course, no movement, not the faintest flicker of a breath, not the tiniest dilation of a pupil – but you remember how I'd had the idea I could read something in the eyes of these paralysed creatures before? Well now I was getting it a hundredfold.

The Doctor knew what was happening.

He knew where he was.

And where he was, was in hell.

I had to do something, and I had to do it straight away. But what? Smash the glass (or perspex, or whatever futuristic material this was)? Didn't think that would work. But then I spotted the little keypad at the top of the cage, and I thought back, and went, 'Aha!' Because I don't know if you remember, but we'd seen Tommy test out one of these things and I had – ooh, how jammy am I?! – I had *memorised the combination*! Ta da!

Five, I typed. Then: seven. Followed by nine, three, one, zero and zero. Finally, with the tiniest of dramatic pauses: eight.

And…

Nothing happened.

I couldn't believe it. Surely each box didn't have its own individual code, *surely*.

I looked again at the Doctor, the pain I saw – imagined? – in his eyes.

I saw a security guard, maybe a few hundred metres away; not looking this way yet, but only a matter of seconds, perhaps, before he noticed the girl trying to get into the restricted cage.

And so I went a little mad. I did everything I could think of, all at once, and to this day I've no idea what bit of it actually worked, what bit of it saved the Doctor but put in motion a series of events that might have killed so many more. It's still on my conscience, you see, and I guess it always will be, although the Doctor says that events were moving inexorably in that direction, and as I wasn't the one who put them in motion in the first place, and I certainly didn't do any of it deliberately, I mustn't blame myself. I get the feeling that he's had to do a lot of justifying to his own conscience over the centuries.

Anyway, I took my collection agent's pendant, and I took the sonic screwdriver, and I put them together, and stuck them in the little keypad, and I pressed every key and threw every likely-looking switch into reverse, and zapped everything with what I imagined to be the screwdriver's 'undoing things' setting.

And everything undid. I mean, *everything*.

The front of the Doctor's cage shimmered away, and he fell over backwards. The first word he said was 'ouch', and the first thing he did was rub his elbow. Then he climbed to his feet, and the look in his eyes – well, that was enough for me. I knew, knew beyond any shadow of a doubt that I'd done the right thing.

Well, for that one second I knew that. And then I realised that I'd done the wrong thing. The totally wrong thing.

There were yells of shock and surprise and alarm from all around. I dragged my gaze from the Doctor, and I saw…

Every creature had disappeared.

Every single one. Every cage had opened, and *every creature was gone!*

My knees buckled under me, and the Doctor jumped forward to catch me.

'What have I done?' I gasped. 'Where've they all gone?'

My knees buckled under me, and the Doctor jumped forward to catch me.

'What have I done?' I gasped. 'What's happened to them?'

But he just shook his head, as wide-eyed as me. 'I don't know,' he said.

I didn't want to let go of him, feeling irrationally that, if I stayed close enough, the bad things would somehow un-happen, like the way your mum proved there had never been monsters under the bed. But I saw security guards stumbling towards us, and knew there were monsters after all.

We began to run through the hordes of headless-chicken visitors, and I realised after a few moments that the Doctor had a destination in mind: the TARDIS. Thank goodness it was still where we'd left it. The Doctor turned the key in the lock and we both fell inside.

I stumbled out an explanation, telling the Doctor what I'd done. 'So – what's happened to all the animals?' I asked again.

He took the pendant from around his neck and began to examine it.

'Oh,' I said in realisation. 'If they're out of suspended animation we can track them, like the rhino.'

The Doctor nodded.

'But we don't have Eve's computer…'

'What's better, Eve's computer or the TARDIS?'

Well, I didn't know how powerful Eve's computer was, but I supposed the TARDIS was a pretty safe bet.

'All the information we need should be in this.' The Doctor plucked the dodo feather out of the console and put his pendant in its place. His fingers twirled across control panels and the column in the centre began to rise and fall. A screen flickered into life and the Doctor perched his glasses on his nose to examine it. 'Ah.'

It didn't sound like a good 'ah' to me. 'What is it?' I asked.

'We're on our way to Earth.' He sighed.

'And that's bad? Come on, you've got to tell me,' I added, as he hesitated.

'I have a theory about what happened,' he said at last. 'Well, I say theory, I'm fairly sure, what with me being, you know, clever and all that. And that destination pretty much confirms it.'

I held my breath, waiting for the worst. But I hadn't suspected quite how bad the worst could be.

'Each specimen is put into suspended animation and teleported directly into a prepared cage, via a pendant. You were trying to open a cage, lift the suspended animation field, and release the… occupant – in other words, more or less reverse the process. The sonic screwdriver enabled you to do that – but it didn't know where to stop. I strongly suspect it amplified the signal, connecting back through the pendant to the central computer, removing all suspended animation fields and feeding inverse coordinates to every animal in a sort of teleportation power surge.'

'You mean…?'

'That all the creatures have ended up back where they came from, yes. Luckily I hadn't been teleported from anywhere, so I wasn't affected.'

But I was still thinking about the other animals. His words had given me the tiniest sliver of hope. 'Back where they originally came from, right. Exactly where they disappeared from. *Exactly*. The same time, I mean,' I added, just to make it absolutely clear.

But he shook his head. 'I don't think so. The museum doesn't have time travel. Not even having the sonic screwdriver in the mix could help out there.'

So I'd sent back billions of extinct animals to twenty-first-century Earth.

'Can we reverse it?' I asked. 'Reverse the reversal, send them back?'

His nose crinkled up. 'Possibly. The question is… even if I can do it, do I want to?'

That didn't make sense. 'You what?'

'Better to die in freedom than live in a cage…' he said.

'Better to be eaten by a dinosaur than live out your normal twenty-first-century life?'

For a second I thought he might argue, but he said, 'Good point.' Then he sort-of smiled. 'Well, let's see what we can do. After all, we like a challenge, don't we, Martha? Something to get our teeth into!'

Talk about unfortunate phrasing. 'And there'll be a load of dinosaurs down there, getting their teeth into people!'

'Old dinosaurs, dying dinosaurs. And the way the land masses have changed, half of them will land in the sea anyway…'

Way to pile on the guilt, Doctor. 'So now I'm the person who wiped out the dinosaurs! Was it a comet, was it climate change, no, it was Martha Jones mucking around with an electronic tool that makes a silly noise!'

The Doctor looked offended at that. 'It's not silly! It's—' He broke off in mid-sonic-screwdriver defence as the TARDIS juddered to a halt.

'But what are we going to do?!' I asked. 'We can't track down 300 billion creatures… can we?' I mean, with a TARDIS, I guessed anything was possible.

'That would be mad!' he said, grinning, which meant he'd been considering the idea. 'Tell you what, though, let's see where the old girl –' he patted the console – 'has brought us while I think up a Plan B.'

Then he turned to me. 'Oh, by the way,' he said. 'Thank you.' The smile slipped for a second and there was an expression so intense I couldn't bear to look at it. I remembered the Chinese girl, how she was willing to do anything to save the person she'd loved. And I realised that whatever I'd done, whatever the consequences might be, I'd dragged the Doctor out of hell. And how could I be sorry for that?

PHORUSRHACOS

Phorusrhacos longissimus

Location: South America

The head of this giant flightless bird is out of proportion to the rest of its body, being a similar size to that of the horse, *equus caballus*. It stands approximately two metres high, and has a large hooked beak. It is a predatory carnivore.

Addendum:

Last reported sighting: 20 million BC.
Cause of extinction: competition for prey due to joining of continents South and North America; climate change.

I-Spyder points value: 800

Creature	Points
Dodo	800
Megatherium	500
Paradise parrot	500
Velociraptor	250
Mountain gorilla	500
Aye-aye	900
Siberian tiger	600
Kakapo	900
Indefatigable Galapagos mouse	1500
Stegosaurus	500
Triceratops	550
Diplodocus	600
Ankylosaurus	650
Dimetrodon	600
Passenger pigeon	100
Thylacine	250
Black rhinoceros	300
Mervin the missing link	23500
Tau duck	5
Dong tao chicken	4
Red-eared slider	40
Chinese three-striped box turtle	350
Forest dragonfly	150
Phorusrhacos	450
Steller's sea cow	1000
Subtotal	35499

ELEVEN

The TARDIS had landed in a cul-de-sac, a narrow side street filled with puddles and rubbish. Martha hurried to the end of the passageway, expecting to see screaming men, women and children running this way and that, arms waving above their heads and eyes wide in terror. But no. The only waving arms belonged to a woman trying to catch the attention of someone the other side of a road, the only wide eyes belonged to a couple of teenage girls watching a couple of teenage boys walk past.

They were in a town – ahead was the high street by the look of things – and almost certainly somewhere in the UK. It wasn't especially futuristic – no hover-cars or moving pavements – and it wasn't at all unrecognisable from places of Martha's own time, there were boutiques, coffee shops and newsagents – although these days, judging by the shop windows, fluorescent green leg warmers were currently in fashion, a cinnamon-orange latte cost €11.50, and some celeb had run off with some other celeb's wife.

The Doctor shut the TARDIS doors and joined her, and they wandered off down the street together.

'So,' said Martha, 'what do we do now? What are we looking for?'

He shrugged. 'The pendant should have given the TARDIS something to work on, should have brought us to a set of relevant coordinates, a place where some creature came from. But could be anything. You know, this would almost certainly have been all forest once. Trees instead of telegraph poles. Bushes instead of bins. And of course whatever was picked up from here originally could be virtually undetectable, could be a microbe, a gnat, a flea…'

'Or that!' Martha rolled her eyes. 'Talk about déjà vu!'

No one else could have spotted it, because it wasn't as if a bizarre-looking bird bigger than a turkey was likely to pass without comment. It was poking its head round a rubbish bin, pushing its enormous hooked beak into a fast-food container that hadn't quite made it inside the receptacle, and seemed remarkably unfazed by the human hustle and bustle surrounding it. It was a dodo.

The Doctor and Martha approached, gingerly. 'Don't scare it!' Martha whispered, creeping forwards on tiptoes.

The dodo didn't run away, just pulled its head out of the cardboard box, spilling ancient French fries across the pavement as it did so, and looked at them with curious eyes as they reached it. Martha came to a halt. 'Now what?' she hissed at the Doctor, not having thought any further than getting as close to it as possible.

'Back to the TARDIS,' he whispered back. 'Keep it safe.'

She held out a hand, with vague thoughts of how you let

dogs or horses sniff you, and the bird waddled towards her, still unafraid. By now one or two people had turned to look, and the Doctor said loudly, 'Ah, there you are, Dorothea. Got lost again! Giant Peruvian flightless homing pigeon,' he added to a staring old lady with a shopping basket on wheels. 'Probably got a bit confused by the one-way system. Come on, girl! Home's this way!'

The dodo – and Martha couldn't fathom why the Doctor had decided to call it Dorothea – stuck close to her side as they made their way back to the TARDIS. There was something else she couldn't work out: 'I thought I'd just put everything in reverse, sent things back to where they came from. But the dodo didn't come from here, it came from Mauritius. And it wasn't found anywhere else, that's what your I-Spyder book says.'

The Doctor nodded. 'Good point. But sailors did carry them off: brought them back home as curiosities, displayed them to the sensation-seeking public for a groat a go. In London in 1638 you could spend a fun afternoon out watching a dodo eat stones as big as nutmegs. Wouldn't be the first species which died out in captivity, not by a long chalk.' His gaze drifted to the middle distance. 'Last ever Tasmanian Tiger, Beaumaris Zoo, 1936. Neglected and starved, she finally froze to death. While troops were slaughtering each other at the start of the Great War, the last ever passenger pigeon was dying in Cincinatti Zoo. I've already told you about the last quagga…'

'Except they weren't the last ones,' Martha pointed out. 'We know what happened to the last-ever quagga.' She shivered, remembering. 'They must have been the penultimate ones. No one would know about the last ever ones, because they'd just… disappear. Zapped off to the museum. Like Dorothea here.'

She reached down and rubbed the creature's downy head.

And then they heard the first scream.

Have you ever been in a situation where things are spiralling horribly, awfully out of control, and you know it's all your fault? I think there are really only two ways to react: be paralysed with fear and guilt, or shove the weight of responsibility to the back of your mind and treat it like you would any other hideous happening. My instinct was to do the former, but I knew I had to force myself to do the latter, because people were going to die.

The Doctor reacts so quickly, it's like it's programmed in. Hear scream, turn and run. Towards it, I mean, not away. As if.

And it's becoming instinctive in me, too. I took a brief, longing look at the still-distant TARDIS, and followed him. Then stopped, reversed, and picked up Dorothea. Then tried to run, found she was too heavy, and stumbled forwards with a kind of lurching trot instead.

There were more and more screams coming now, suddenly joined by the piercing screech of a fire alarm. We rounded a corner, and were nearly knocked over by a crowd of people running the other way, but there was no sign of a fire. In front of us was a supermarket, with screaming shoppers streaming out of the automatic doors, dropping their carrier bags in panic and sending apples and oranges and frozen ready meals sliding away in all directions. One woman was yelling 'A bear, a bear!', another was crying 'A tiger!' and a spotty teenage boy in a pastel yellow supermarket uniform was shouting about 'A monster!'

By the time I got there, the doors were just hissing shut behind the Doctor. Seconds later, they slid open again for me. I crept in cautiously – mind you, I could have been wearing hobnailed boots for all you could hear above the alarm – but I was unable to see where he'd got to, or where the bear/tiger/monster was, for that matter. Dorothea looked around curiously as I tiptoed down the fruit and veg aisle, stretching out her neck to snag a bunch of grapes in her enormous beak.

We were creeping past the deli counter when I heard a crash. I hurried as fast as I could towards it, trying not to slip on the tins of peaches and pears that were rolling across the floor. Round the corner, I could see why the fleeing customers had been confused. The creature was the size and shape of a bear, but with the tawny coat and feline face of a big cat.

It also had the largest set of fangs I'd ever seen, like a couple of bony bananas sticking out of its mouth.

And the Doctor was standing right in front of it.

I yelped. 'Is that a sabre-toothed tiger?'

The Doctor looked in my direction. 'Yes. Interesting, isn't it? Because there's no way the last one could have crossed the Atlantic and ended up here.'

Yes, Doctor, now was definitely the time to be worrying about how it arrived thousands of years ago, rather than that it was HERE, NOW!

I edged closer nervously and saw that the Doctor was holding up the sonic screwdriver, waving it in the animal's face. It was shaking its furry head from side to side, as if trying to dislodge a buzzing bee from inside its skull. Behind it crouched a couple of old ladies, tea-cosy hats on their heads, obviously far too scared to attempt to pass the beast.

The Doctor used the non-sonic-screwdriver-holding hand to wave me away. 'Get out while you can,' he said. 'This won't hold it for long, I've just confused it for a few moments. Trying to give people time to get away. The sabre-tooth is built for ambush, not catching prey on the run – if they get enough of a head start, they should be OK.'

One of the old ladies whimpered. 'Go on,' he urged me again, then called out, 'Don't worry. It'll be all right,' in a cheerfully reassuring voice that was almost drowned out by the sound of sirens from outside. I turned to look through the glass store front, and could see two great big fire engines drawing up. Firemen jumped down and the automatic doors swished open to let them into the shop. They saw the sabre-tooth. They ran out again.

All except one, a tall, moustached black man. 'No fire, then,' he called out to the Doctor – and I won't say he didn't sound scared, but I guess he was the kind of man who didn't let being scared get in the way.

'No fire,' the Doctor called back. 'I won't say it was exactly a false alarm, but…'

'What can I do to help?' the fireman yelled over the sound not only of the bell, but also of one of the fire engines hastily reversing away outside.

I nudged the Doctor. I could see that the tiger was

beginning to focus, wasn't shaking its head anywhere near so violently. We might not have very long.

'Right!' said the Doctor, all firm and decisive. 'As soon as the spell breaks, I'll try to lead it out. Could you, er…?'

'Albert.'

'Albert, you see to Agnes and Millicent here. But make sure you're not in its path.' I could see the Doctor was worried. How much easier for the animal to turn on sitting prey rather than chase after a running target.

And Albert got the idea too. He nodded, and before the Doctor could say another word he had leapt onto a chiller cabinet and was inching along, making his way to the other side of the tiger, to where the two old ladies were huddled together. 'Be careful!' I shrieked, ridiculously – I mean, as if you weren't going to be careful when you were climbing over a deadly prehistoric predator.

He jumped down the other side and, after a breathless hello to the women, began grabbing packets and tins, building a barrier between them and the animal. Even worried as he was, I saw half a grin on the Doctor's face – this was his kind of man.

'How did the sabre-tooth die out?' I asked, hoping for a clue. I mean, I know we couldn't – shouldn't – kill the last member of an otherwise extinct species, but if it was it or me…

'Climate change, leading to vegetation change, leading to prey change, leading to no food,' the Doctor replied. 'Probably.'

'So not a solution we could utilise in the next two minutes, then,' I said – as the tiger took a step towards us.

The Doctor began to pull packets of bacon out of the chiller, ripping them open and draping the rashers over his shoulders. He had, I decided, gone totally loopy. 'Might help if I really smell of meat!' he told me. 'Entice him in this direction!'

Yes, loopy. Noble, but loopy.

'Now, Martha, run!' he yelled at me. And I decided that this time, it really was a good idea to do as he said.

I stumbled down the aisle towards the exit, swerving round abandoned groceries and pushing my way through 'Five items or less'. 'Faster!' the Doctor was yelling, not seeming to appreciate the fact that I was carrying a bird the size of a sheep. And I wasn't going to leave her – but, on the other hand, I didn't want to be ripped to pieces by a sabre-toothed tiger either. What to do?

At that moment, just as my head was about to explode (and my lungs too, come to that), I spotted the solution. Two seconds later, Dorothea was happily sat in a supermarket trolley, and I was dashing down the road pushing it like a demented contestant on *Supermarket Sweep*.

The Doctor caught me up as I passed the remaining fire engine. 'Is it coming?' I gasped.

'Oh yes. Albert and the others'll be fine.'

'Good,' I replied, although, selfish as it may sound, I was at that exact second more worried about me. 'What now?' I asked.

'Oh, I'll think of something,' the Doctor said, filling me with no confidence whatsoever.

A roar came from behind and I upped my speed. 'Are you sure they can't sprint?'

'They're not built for speed over long distances,' he reassured me, strewing bacon on the path as he ran to try to distract the creature. 'Bummer for them when their habitat turned to desert, no trees to lurk behind for an ambush…' And I could almost hear ideas stirring inside his head as we turned into the high street. 'Martha! Do you know why people of your time knew so much about an extinct animal from the Ice Age?'

'No,' I panted, fighting to keep the trolley on a straight path as its wheels wanted to go all over the place.

'The reason is, thousands of 'em were preserved in the La Brea tar pits in what became Los Angeles. Bison wanders in, gets stuck, tiger thinks "aha! Easy prey", goes in after it and gets stuck too. Sinks into the goo and dies.'

'Hurrah,' I said, as sarcastically as I could manage through the shortness of breath. 'Lucky there're some good old English tar pits just down the road.'

'Yes!' he said. 'Well spotted! Down on the road…'

He stopped dead. Which I thought was about to become literally true, because the tiger, not to be sidetracked by some slices of dead pig, was gaining on us. We had seconds.

The Doctor stood in the middle of the road, sonic screwdriver raised. But we knew that only worked for a few moments!

'Doctor!' I screamed as the sabre-tooth bounded towards us, closer, closer…

As I watched in panic, though, I saw that he was doing something different this time. Where the screwdriver was pointing at the road, the top layer was beginning to bubble. The tarmac surface was melting…

The sabre-tooth leapt – and landed on the sticky tar. Its paws started to sink – and the Doctor twiddled the screwdriver's controls; the surface stopped bubbling, started solidifying again. Seconds later, the tiger was trapped, up to its furry ankles in what the Mafia would probably call tarmac overshoes. It roared furiously.

Now what? 'We're not taking that back to the TARDIS too, are we?' I asked the Doctor, as we stood watching the angry animal. I still felt a bit shivery.

'Don't think it would fit through the cat flap,' he replied. 'And I bet it's not house tr—'

Then a familiar voice came from behind us, interrupting the Doctor. 'You beat me to it!'

I turned. There was a figure in MOTLO green overalls, a pendant in his hands and a relieved expression on his bearded face. Tommy.

SABRE-TOOTHED TIGER

Smilodon fatalis

Location: North America

The most distinctive feature of the sabre-toothed tiger is its two upper canine teeth. These sabre-like blades are about 17 centimetres long, tapering to a serrated point. It has a heavy, muscular body with a thick chest. Its tail is short and it has retractile claws. It preys on large herbivores such as bison.

Addendum:

Last reported sighting: *c.*9000 BC.
Probable cause of extinction: loss of prey due to climate change.

I-Spyder points value: 500

Creature	Points
Dodo	800
Megatherium	500
Paradise parrot	500
Velociraptor	250
Mountain gorilla	500
Aye-aye	900
Siberian tiger	600
Kakapo	900
Indefatigable Galapagos mouse	1500
Stegosaurus	500
Triceratops	550
Diplodocus	600
Ankylosaurus	650
Dimetrodon	600
Passenger pigeon	100
Thylacine	250
Black rhinoceros	300
Mervin the missing link	23500
Tau duck	5
Dong tao chicken	4
Red-eared slider	40
Chinese three-striped box turtle	350
Forest dragonfly	150
Phorusrhacos	450
Steller's sea cow	1000
Sabre-toothed tiger	500
Subtotal	35999

TWELVE

Tommy jogged towards the Doctor and Martha, darting glances at the static sabre-tooth. 'Well done!' he said. 'Everything's gone mad, the signals are cutting out as soon as they're received. I'd given up hope of tracking anything at all—' He broke off, staring at Martha's shopping trolley, and a frown spread across his face. The Earther held up his pendant, shaking it like a stopped watch. 'Damn, I thought that meant things were working properly again, but it must still be on the blink. It says there's only one specimen in the area, and it's pointing in another direction entirely.' He shrugged. 'Well, I can take them both back anyway…'

Martha pulled the dodo back as he tried to take it. A feather fluttered to the floor, which the Doctor picked up. 'Don't take her,' Martha said. 'Please.'

Tommy raised an eyebrow. 'Why not? Come on, Martha, do you know how much damage has been done to the collection? We need to get as many specimens back as soon as possible!'

She shook her head. 'If that much damage has been done,' she said, and couldn't suppress a guilty shudder, 'then one more or less here or there isn't going to make much difference, is it?' Down by her knees, Dorothea gave a little squawk, and Martha leaned over to pat her on the beak. 'I don't want her back in one of your cages. Not yet. She's happy with me. Let her live a little.'

'Until a dinosaur gets her, or one of the Earth natives decides to stick her in a freak show, or she tries to cross the road in front of one of those cars they didn't have a few hundred years ago when she was last around.'

Martha refused to let him wind her up. 'Yeah. Except those things aren't going to happen, cos I'm looking after her.'

They locked gazes for a few moments, each intolerant of the other's point of view, but it was Tommy who dropped his eyes first. He didn't look happy but, as his only other option was to take the bird by force, Martha thought she'd won the point for the time being. Still, probably best not to take her eye off Dorothea while any Earther was around from now on.

The Doctor broke the tension – well, in a way, his question made Martha feel more tense than ever. 'So, what's going on up there?' he asked Tommy. 'Back in everyone's favourite Museum of the Last Ones.'

'You know what happened?' Tommy said. The Doctor nodded. Martha couldn't bring herself to. 'The entire Earth section was affected, but nowhere else. We still don't know what caused it – some massive power surge is what they're saying.' (Guilt made Martha's stomach flip-flop worse than if she'd been on a roller-coaster at Alton Towers, but there was a sense of relief there too – 'only' the Earth section. Not all the museum. OK, that was still billions of creatures, but…) 'Whether Eve has more of a clue about it than the rest of us I've no idea,' Tommy continued. 'She's practically had a breakdown over this.' Well, it served her right for trying to trap the Doctor. Martha tried to keep that in mind, rather than thinking of everything else that her actions had achieved…

'Has she really?' the Doctor was replying when Martha focused again. 'A breakdown, you say?'

Tommy nodded. 'Well, MOTLO is her life's work. OK, so the Earth section's only a small part of it, but even so…'

And she'd lost the last of the Time Lords too. But neither the Doctor nor Martha was going to enlighten Tommy about that.

Tommy shook his head sadly. 'Of course, it means a lot to all of us, but to Eve – well, she's been there for ever. Her life's work, like I said.'

The Doctor's head jerked up then, a flash of interest in his eyes, like something had just occurred to him. 'Her life's work. Yes. Do you know, I wonder if it really is.'

'What do you mean?' Martha asked.

'I'm just wondering,' he replied, 'quite how long Eve has worked at the museum for.'

This interesting question didn't seem to concern Tommy, who was now heading towards the still-struggling sabre-toothed tiger. 'Not got any objections to me taking this one back, Martha?' he said. She shook her head. Not that the tiger didn't deserve a few moments of freedom as much as the dodo, she supposed, but… Well, it was easier to feel sympathy towards something that didn't want to eat you.

Tommy continued walking towards the creature, pendant held in his outstretched hand, completely unafraid.

Martha and the Doctor, watching, were unafraid too. They knew by now how the pendants worked, whether they agreed with the procedure or not. First the animal would be immobilised. Then it would be zapped straight to its museum prison, into its cell.

So not one of them thought for a second that Tommy was in danger. And it took a second to realise what was happening, as he raised the pendant, as nothing happened. As the tiger sank its enormous canines into his side.

Tommy collapsed to the pavement and the Doctor leapt forwards, fumbling for his sonic screwdriver, Martha at his heels, her medical instincts having kicked in immediately. As they got close, the Doctor waved his little metal device at the tiger like a magic wand. Snarling resentfully, the beast pulled its head back. The Doctor held his position, keeping the creature at bay.

Martha threw herself down on the pavement beside Tommy. To her enormous relief, a few checks showed he was still alive, although he was bleeding heavily. Nervously aware of the fearsome creature towering over her – and remembering that the ultrasonics of the screwdriver hadn't kept it quiet for that long before – she set to work, staunching the bleeding and making Tommy comfortable.

'He'll be OK,' she said to the Doctor after a few minutes, still concentrating on her patient. 'But he should get to a hospital. I mean, he'll need a tetanus shot at the very least.

Who knows what sort of bacteria there might be on the teeth of a ten-thousand-year-old tiger?'

The Doctor didn't reply, and she looked up then. He was still holding out the sonic screwdriver, still keeping the tiger away from Tommy, but his head was turned away, staring in the other direction.

Martha stared too.

'I spy with my little eye, something beginning with M,' the Doctor said after a second.

'You mean D,' said Martha, in a flat, puzzled voice as she saw what he was looking at.

'No no no. M. I'm talking about one great big mmm-mystery.'

And Martha couldn't help but agree. Because there in a shop doorway was another dodo.

I looked back over my shoulder. Dorothea was still in the shopping trolley, happily shredding stray carrier bags with the point of her mad beak to form a sort of nest.

I turned the other way again. There, scrabbling through a pile of abandoned *Big Issues*, was what could have been her twin.

Two dodos. Which wasn't possible. One specimen of everything, the museum had. Just the one.

Except…

There was another sabre-toothed tiger coming down the high street.

Mystery upon mystery. The evidence was mounting up that something dodgy was going on. Two dodos when the museum only had one. Two tigers when the museum only had one. Tommy had thought there was only one 'specimen' in the area. His pendant didn't freeze the tiger. So, yes, lots of evidence, lots of ooh-er-it's-a-mystery – but, quite frankly, just at that moment I wanted to deal with the not-dying first and do the detective thing later.

We couldn't just run, not with an unconscious and injured man at our feet. We couldn't get back to the TARDIS, because the second sabre-tooth was between it and us. At the moment the sonic screwdriver was keeping it at a distance, but it was making tentative steps forward and it was pretty clear that it wouldn't keep working for long.

And then I saw something even more bizarre. I grabbed the Doctor's arm and pointed.

'Mm, interesting,' said the Doctor, responding to my 'ooh ooh ooh' and frantic indications in the direction of the dodo. He whipped his glasses out of his pocket and balanced them on his nose, peering distantly at the bird and what it was doing. 'Yes, I'd definitely say that was interesting.'

Actually, this was all turning into interesting overload. Because just then, as I gazed over the Doctor's shoulder, I spotted something else. I'll try to explain our position, because it's probably getting a bit complicated for you to follow: imagine a nice high street lined with shops. In the middle of the street see three people, a supermarket trolley with a dodo in it, and an angrily trapped sabre-toothed tiger. The Doctor is waving his sonic screwdriver between that tiger and another one that's approaching from the right. That's your right as you're imagining this, not his right; it would have been his right a few moments ago, but now he's facing you with the screwdriver behind his back, as he stares at the dodo. For the purposes of our imaginary plan, you're pretty much standing on the dodo. Ooh, almost forgot, way behind the second tiger (to your right, remember) you can see the TARDIS, a little square blue shape in the distance.

Right, the Doctor's looking towards you, and I'm looking a bit to your left, where there's an electricals shop. I'm nudging the Doctor again, and now he's looking there too. We start to edge a bit closer, but we can't go too far because the Doctor has to keep the tiger away from Tommy, who's still unconscious on the ground.

So, this shop – the window's all full of futuristic tellies, all enormous flat screens and 3-D. That would have caught my eye anyway, but my gaze was dragged towards what the screens were showing: a news report I guess, although a few days ago I would have assumed it to be an action movie. The scene changed rapidly between horrors, some all too familiar – more sabre-toothed tigers on the rampage with people fleeing left and right, worse still, little two-legged dinosaurs running wild. 'What are they?' I said.

'Look it up in the *I-Spyder* guide,' the Doctor said, and I'd actually got as far as getting out the book when I realised that it didn't exactly matter; all that mattered was that they had very sharp teeth and claws. 'You look,' I said, pushing the book at the Doctor.

He took it, but something else on the screen had got his attention. His glasses came out again and he was leaning forwards, concentrating hard. He'd spotted something. I couldn't tell what, but he nodded for me to go a bit closer, so I did – and then I saw it too.

In almost every scene, somewhere, in the background,

or the foreground, or somewhere off to the side, there was a plump grey-white bird, big of beak and perky of tail feather. A dodo. That was weird enough. But what made it even odder was that, just like the one in front of us (the one you're standing on), they all seemed to be scrabbling at the ground. In some of the pictures, a white sphere was visible at their feet.

'They've got eggs,' I said. 'And they're burying them. Do you think there's some weird plan going on to repopulate the Earth with dodos?'

'You mean, someone's sending sabre-toothed tigers and dinosaurs to clear the way for our feathered friends? Bit extreme, don't you think?'

I huffed. 'Well, what do you think's going on?'

'Oh, bound to be something far more sinister.'

Now I sighed as I took the few steps backwards needed to join him again. 'Isn't it always? Come on, then, give us a clue.'

'Ah,' he said. 'Well, there's another clue heading this way. But I'm not sure you'd want it, even for a present.'

I looked where he was pointing – down the street to your left. There was a dinosaur. Not one of the ones like on the shop's tellies – they were only (ha, 'only'!) about six feet long and this was at least half that again, standing upright like a Tyrannosaurus, with a huge head and, ooh, *ee-nor-mous* pointed teeth.

Amazing how calmly I'm telling you all that. Oh, here comes a dinosaur. Here comes something ready, willing and able to bite me in half in a second, and, ooh look, there's no escape. The sonic's not going to work on tigers and dinosaurs, is it? And like I said before, we can't run away, not with an unconscious man at our feet.

Talking of whom, I knelt down to check his progress. He wasn't making any. 'I would have hoped he'd be waking up by now,' I said to the Doctor. 'Really, he needs to get to a hospital, be checked out properly.'

The Doctor's answer didn't seem to be an answer at all, at first. 'This is obviously something to do with MOTLO,' he said. Well, yeah, even I'd figured that one out. Thanks, Doctor.

'So we need to find out what's going on there. What's with the tigers and dodos and dinosaurs.' Couldn't disagree there.

'And Tommy needs help, which we can't get for him.' Again, so much stating the obvious, but at least veering in the direction of my question. 'Give me your pendant a second.'

I did so, not quite sure what he wanted it for.

'So, this is what's going to happen. You're going back to the museum, you're going to get help for Tommy, and you're going to find out what's going on while I deal with these wee beasties down here. OK?' He began to programme numbers into the pendant's keypad.

Hang on a minute…

Before I really knew what was happening, the Doctor had shoved the shopping trolley towards me and, as I grabbed at it instinctively, he flung the pendant's cord back over my head. Then with a twisty-turny move that would impress any yoga guru, he bent over to push the big blue buttons on both mine and Tommy's pendants and suddenly…

I was back in the Earth section of MOTLO, Tommy at my feet and the Dorothea-containing trolley by my side, knowing that the Doctor was light years away, still surrounded by deadly prehistoric creatures.

I wasn't happy. But he'd given me a job to do, so I was going to do it. I'd pretty much figured out by now that that was how this whole deal worked.

DROMAEOSAURUS

Dromaeosaurus albertensis

Location: North America

Dromaeosaurus is a carnivorous theropod dinosaur of just under two metres in length. It walks on its hind legs, which are relatively short, but powerful. The centre toe on each of its three-toed feet has a long, sickle-shaped claw. Its body is covered with structures that resemble feathers.

Addendum:

Last reported sighting: late Cretaceous period. Cause of extinction: environmental change.

I-Spyder points value: 200

THIRTEEN

The vast Earth section was still empty of creatures as far as the eye could see – Dorothea the dodo aside – and devoid now of visitors too. 'Hello?' Martha called, quietly at first, slightly intimidated by the space and the silence, and then louder and louder as no response was forthcoming. Yes, she supposed she was a fugitive, but Tommy's safety was more important right now. She self-consciously did a little jog around just in case the movement sensors had been switched on, but no alarm sounded.

Having given Tommy a quick check – he was still stable, if not exactly in the best of health – she set off to look for help. It was harder to navigate without the animal landmarks, but signs still stood at most junctions, pointing hopelessly towards a non-existent parrot or panda, and that helped.

Suddenly – whether it was seeing a sign indicating the Black Rhino, or whether she would have remembered anyway – her memory was jogged. The pendants – they could be used to communicate too! Her first instinct was to make her way back to Tommy and then call for help, but she realised that actually it suited her purpose more to be somewhere else, keep out of the clutches of the security guards and remain a free agent. Or Agent. She'd become Agent Jones again because, after all, she had some detecting to do.

She examined the pendant around her neck and found the appropriate switch. 'Medical assistance required,' she hissed into it. 'Earther down, Earther down! Earth section, er...' She tried to remember what signs she'd seen by their arrival point, and checked her pocket for the *I-Spyder* guide to see if she'd got the name right – but of course the Doctor still had that. Which meant that she couldn't update it. Not that that mattered – the vast emptiness surrounding her meant her accumulation of points had just come to an abrupt halt. 'Near where the Kosher Cake was,' she attempted.

'The Kosrae Crake?' came a voice in return, possibly Rix's. Then, in a more perturbed tone, 'Hang on, who is this?'

'Never mind that. Just help Tommy.' Then she firmly pushed the switch into its 'off' position.

She crept through the deserted halls, pushing the supermarket trolley in front of her, trying to ignore its squeaky wheel, trying to ignore thoughts of the Doctor millions of miles away, facing down a dinosaur.

In a funny kind of way, the Doctor was quite pleased. After all, merely being surrounded by sabre-toothed tigers wasn't much of a challenge when he'd already figured out how to stop them – the old road-melting trick didn't have to be a one-off. So, a dinosaur in the mix at least made things a bit more interesting. At the very least, running away from it while simultaneously trapping tigers added some spice to the mix.

The dinosaur trod on a pillar box, squashing it flat, an action that would cause a number of bills to remain unpaid, some birthdays to be left uncelebrated, and a promising romance to be broken off amid a storm of rows and allegations.

The Doctor was dodging here and there, sonic screwdriver waving frantically to and fro as he liquefied this bit of tarmac, reformed that bit, avoided teeth and ducked out of the reach of claws – all the while trying to keep a significant distance between himself and the dinosaur.

So far, there was only one dinosaur; no others of the same kind had turned up, either in the town or – as far as he could see – on TV. That was also interesting. Because perhaps this was the real thing, the actual 'specimen' that both the TARDIS and Tommy had tracked down. Although the Doctor had sent Martha back to the museum to find out what was going on, he did already have a few ideas about some of it, and one of those ideas was that the duplicate animals were not genuine exhibits from the Museum of the Last Ones. If they were not 'specimens', it would explain why Tommy had not been able to zap the sabre-toothed tiger – but if this was the real deal, a Last One whose details were in the Museum's central computer, then it could be immobilised. And he just happened to have one of the pendants in the TARDIS. Not programmed for this particular creature, of course, but such petty details hardly worried the owner of a sonic screwdriver.

The Doctor had a sudden thought. He hadn't returned the *I-Spyder* guide to Martha, it was still in his pocket. Doing several things at once was second nature to the Doctor, and he kept running while he brought up the book's prehistoric reptile section, feeding in as many details of the dinosaur as he could to narrow down the selection. Aha! There it was. Megalosaurus. And it had been a native of these parts. So the likelihood of it being genuine was fairly high. Good.

He looked up from the book's screen. He was just approaching the side street where the TARDIS had landed. And there in front of him was another sabre-toothed tiger. He raised the screwdriver again, but there was no tarmac to melt, just paving slabs. He turned. The Megalosaurus was just clearing the coffee shop. He was between a rock and a hard place. No, actually that sounded a lot more attractive than his real situation. Just leave it that he was between a fierce, huge, deadly prehistoric killer, and an even fiercer and more huge deadly prehistoric killer.

The sabre-tooth got nearer. The Megalosaurus got nearer. Nearer and nearer. Escape options flashed into the Doctor's head but were instantly rejected, each leaving him further away from the TARDIS and not significantly safer anyway.

Nearer. Nearer. The Megalosaurus lunged. The sabre-tooth lunged. The Doctor took a deep breath… as the two monsters sank their teeth into each other.

Round and round the creatures span, a fearsome whirlwind of teeth and talons. The Doctor, breath let out, hovered on the outskirts, trying to sense an opening that might lead him to the TARDIS, but the fight was between him and the alleyway entrance.

The dinosaur was winning, the big cat tiring as blood poured from the wounds of tooth and claw. With one final, moribund effort, the sabre-tooth lashed out and the Megalosaurus stepped back – into the mouth of the cul-de-sac. The cul-de-sac where the TARDIS was. The cul-de-sac that was really too narrow for an enormous dinosaur.

The Doctor watched in consternation as the tiger breathed its last. The Megalosaurus tried to move forward again – but it was stuck fast, wedged in between two buildings. It seemed temporarily unconcerned, pacified by the corpse of the unfortunate sabre-tooth which it proceeded to tear to shreds, but the Doctor wasn't so calm. He had to get to the TARDIS. He needed a way over the dinosaur – but, unlike Albert in the supermarket, he had no handy chiller cabinets to climb on. Not that they made chiller cabinets that tall…

Albert! Of course! The Doctor suddenly had an idea. He hared off down the road, doubling back on himself.

Yes! There outside the supermarket a fire engine still stood. A fire engine with a ladder on the top…

He opened a door and climbed up, schoolboy pleasure at being inside such a machine blotting out all worries about the present crisis. He flexed his wrists and grasped the steering wheel, a big grin on his face.

A throat was cleared on the other side of the door. The Doctor looked out of the window. 'I think you might need this,' said Albert, holding up a key.

The Doctor reached out, but Albert didn't hand it over. 'What's up?' he asked.

'I need the ladder,' the Doctor told him. 'To climb over a dinosaur.'

'Ladder needs two people to operate,' said Albert. 'Shove over.'

'Do you know how to drive this thing, then?'

'I'm the man with the key,' Albert said. 'Why d'you think the rest all went off on the other appliance? Course I know how to drive it.'

The Doctor looked crestfallen. 'I was sort of hoping you didn't,' he said. 'I don't suppose…'

'Nope,' said Albert, grinning. 'Tell you what, though, maybe on the way back. After we've sorted the dinosaur.'

The Doctor returned the grin, moving over to let Albert into the driving seat. 'It's a deal!'

To the Doctor's disappointment, Albert wouldn't let him put on the sirens or the flashing blue lights as they drove down the road towards the Megalosaurus. 'You really want to alert that thing?' the fireman asked, which the Doctor had to admit was a good point. The dinosaur didn't pay any attention to them as they pulled up, though, still being occupied with its sabre-toothed meal. But how long it would remain distracted for was the question.

'Yup, that's a big beast all right,' commented Albert matter-of-factly as he pulled on the brake. 'Lucky it's a big ladder…

The fireman showed the Doctor how to use the system of ropes and pulleys that extended the ladder upwards. They were both uncomfortably aware as they worked that the merest flick of a claw could prove their undoing, should the dinosaur switch its attention to them.

'Any particular reason you need to climb over the thing?' Albert asked as they began hauling away.

'Got a time machine the other side,' the Doctor said.

'Oh,' said Albert.

Soon the ladder was fully extended. The Doctor made Albert get back into the vehicle's cab, with strict instructions to drive away should the Megalosaurus become an immediate danger – no matter what position the Doctor was in. Then he began to climb.

The dinosaur's head was lowered, attacking the tiger corpse, but it was still a formidable height. The Doctor reached the top – just as a huge eye flickered towards him.

The head reared up. Jaws opened. The Doctor leapt…

… And landed on the creature's scaly forehead. He scrambled upwards as a forearm flailed worryingly near, but then he was over the top and sliding down the other side, like he was in the *Flintstones* title sequence. The TARDIS key was in his hand ready, and he slid off the end of the tail and inserted the key in one flowing movement. He grabbed the pendant out of its slot on the console, zip zap zipped with the sonic screwdriver, and was back through the doors in seconds. Were his calculations correct? Would it work?

Yes. The dinosaur froze, and the Doctor breathed a sigh of relief. But now what? Could he reverse the reversal, Martha had asked; send the creatures back? Well, he had a pendant, and he had the sonic screwdriver. He didn't have access to the museum's central computer, but he did have the TARDIS.

Send the creatures *back*…

The Doctor thought about a few things. Having thought about them, he smiled broadly.

* * *

Albert, poised over the wheel of the fire engine, was staring hard at the Megalosaurus when suddenly there was no Megalosaurus there to stare at. He blinked once or twice, then shrugged. Dinosaur, no dinosaur, that was just the way things went. Behind where the dinosaur had been was a blue box, tall in its way but not a quarter of the height of the enormous reptile.

The Doctor emerged from the doorway of the blue box, and waved cheerfully to Albert. Albert waved back.

'All done,' the Doctor told him, jogging back to the appliance. 'Well, I say all, I've still got a few billion extinct animals to sort out as well as various probable clones, not to mention picking up my companion from a space museum while avoiding the megalomaniacal proprietor who wants to turn me into an exhibit.'

'Is that right?' asked Albert.

The Doctor nodded. 'But first…' he said. 'If I drive it round the block, may I put the siren on this time, *please*?'

MEGALOSAURUS

Megalosaurus bucklandi

Location: Eurasia (addendum: areas later
known as England and France)

The carnivorous Megalosaurus is a large
theropod dinosaur, similar in appearance to
Tyrannosaurus rex, although half its size – it is
about 9 metres long and 3 metres in height. It
walks upright and has relatively small arms and
a long, heavy tail.

Addendum:

Last reported sighting: Jurassic period.
Cause of extinction: environmental changes.

I-Spyder points value: 400

FOURTEEN

I heard people coming, and looked for somewhere to hide. Of course, had I not zapped all the dinosaurs to modern-day Earth, that would have been easy enough, but as it was… I crouched behind a sign indicating the way to the gift shop, put a finger to my lips and *shhh*ed at Dorothea, and hoped for the best.

The footsteps got louder. There was also the sound of something being wheeled along and for a moment I thought they'd got a shopping trolley too, but as I peered cautiously around the sign I saw that it was actually a wheeled stretcher. The men pushing it wore jumpsuits with 'Infirmary' written on the back, and on the stretcher lay Tommy. There was colour in his cheeks and he was breathing normally and, although I wasn't really in any position to make a prognosis, I was pretty sure he was going to be all right. Didn't stop me feeling bad for abandoning him, though – but I didn't have time to indulge in guilt; I had a job to do. Or try to do…

It's all very well being sent to find out something. But

when you actually come to consider the matter, you realise it's not quite as simple as that. Size of museum: probably several million square miles; size of investigator: well, I might manage six feet if I was wearing high heels and standing on a stool. Like looking for a needle in a haystack as big as Wales. Except more difficult, because at least you'd know (a) that you were searching for a needle, and (b) what a needle looks like. Because I didn't have a clue what I was after.

Duplicate dodos, double dinosaurs, same sabre-tooths. Someone had to be breeding them – or, more likely, this being the future and everything, cloning them. That would account for them being identical.

I looked down at Dorothea. I guessed this meant she wasn't the last dodo after all – that was probably back on Mauritius right now, causing havoc among the holidaymakers – but something grown in a vat from an abstracted cell or two. Did it make her any less of a being? Not in my eyes. I ruffled her neck feathers, and she nuzzled my hand, seemingly perfectly content in my company. I guess, like her earlier relatives, she'd not experienced any predators inside her vat, didn't know that humans could bring harm. She'd known nothing except a laboratory before her brief foray on to the Earth.

She'd known nothing except a laboratory…

'Giant Peruvian flightless homing pigeon', the Doctor had called the bird to cunningly mislead a curious passer-by. And the 'Dodo' entry in the *I-Spyder* guide had called it 'the largest member of the pigeon family'. Could it be possible…? Was there any chance whatsoever that the Doctor's jesting words had contained a grain of truth…?

I waited until the infirmary party was completely out of sight, and then hefted Dorothea out of the trolley. She started walking forwards and I held my breath, but she'd only gone to investigate an empty paper cup, presumably dropped by a visitor.

I breathed out. It had been a daft idea. Time to rethink.

Here's what I've found is useful, being a detective – OK, being with the Doctor – coming up with ridiculous, pie-in-the-sky hypotheses and not being afraid to test them. Where was all this stuff happening? That's right, Earth. Therefore who was most likely to be involved? Yup, one of the Earthers. After all, one of them had already been exposed as a dodgy dealer. I considered Frank as the culprit. Possible, but he was currently locked up, so how could he have sent all the clones to Earth? Plus, would he have the scientific knowledge necessary to create them in the first place?

Still, the Earthers' quarters seemed as good a place as any to start the search. Of course, I didn't know where they were. I did, however, know which cafeteria door Vanni had gone out of on her way to bed, and I couldn't think of any other starting point. So I put Dorothea back in the trolley and set off. I didn't have the instincts of a homing pigeon, but I was fairly sure I could find the way to the cafeteria, mainly because there were signs with great big arrows indicating the right direction.

The sight of the canteen made me realise that I'd only had a doughnut all day, and I was starving. Of course, I didn't have any money on me to get something out of the vending machines. Then I spotted a cardboard box by the side of a half-empty machine. Refills?

Funny how your polite, twenty-first-century, law-abiding habits are hard to break. Could I bring myself to nick a packet of crisps? Not at first. And then I reminded myself that thanks to this museum I'd been nearly shot and nearly eaten, to name but two incidents, so the least it owed me was a packet of cheese and onion. So I had one, with some salt and vinegar to follow, and bother the cholesterol. I did venture a sniff at a packet of sausage and marshmallow, obviously the in-flavour of the future, but chickened out. They turned out to be a hit with Dorothea, though, who crunched the savoury-sweet snack down with every indication of enjoyment.

She was halfway through the crisps when she suddenly stopped, and put her head to one side. Listening? Birds must have ears, mustn't they, it's just you can't see them. Yes, of course they have, there'd be no point in all that chirping otherwise. Anyway, after listening for a few moments, she waddled to the end of the trolley, pushing on the child seat as if trying to propel the whole thing forward – but owing to physics she couldn't, of course.

I lifted her out, hardly daring to breath. Surely my plan wasn't actually working?! Was she really 'homing'?

She waddled off, and I followed eagerly.

Through the door, down a corridor, down another corridor. Then she stopped outside what appeared to be a plain white wall and started scrabbling at it with her beak. I listened. There were definite squawking sounds coming from the other side of the wall. Dorothea probably hadn't been homing, she'd just been following the sounds. 'Just.' Well, it was good enough for me. But how to get in when there didn't seem to be any doors at all… Not for the first time, I wished I had a sonic screwdriver of my own.

Then, suddenly, a section of the wall slid back. I don't know who was more surprised, me or Frank.

Frank. There you are, always go with your first instinct.

'You're supposed to be locked up!' I cried.

He took a couple of steps back. 'Yeah, right. Ain't built a place yet that can hold me.'

'What are you doing?' I asked.

He shrugged, defensively. 'Just nipping out for a – well, you know.'

There, planning advice for anyone thinking of installing a secret laboratory with secret doors – make sure it's got a loo. If Frank had done that, he'd probably be free to this day.

'That's not what I meant,' I told him, and before he could stop me I'd pushed past.

If I was going to find any answers, this looked like the place to be.

Martha gazed around the room, fascinated. Unlike the grotty warehouse where they'd found the rhino, this was a gleaming laboratory, much more in accord with her ideas of what places should look like in the future. There were benches covered with test tubes – about the only scientific equipment that even medical Martha recognised among the vast array of gizmos and gadgets. Behind a desk was a bank of screens, the images too small for her to make out at a distance. There was a variety of creatures, at a variety of life stages, including a pen of dodo chicks, next to a pen of dodo adolescents, next to a pen of fully grown Dorothea lookalikes. Dorothea herself waddled over and rubbed her beak against the wire mesh, eliciting a flurry of flapping feathers and squawks in return. The far wall contained a couple of metal doors solid with bolts – snarls and roars gave Martha a clue as to what could be found behind them.

She'd been right: all those identical animals on Earth, they were clones.

And then she got it, and a rush of relief swept through her: 'Those animals you were selling off – they were clones too! You weren't destroying the Last Ones.' (She fought down the little accusatory voice inside that said: 'Not like you. Not like you did.') 'That's why there were those double entries on the warehouse computer.'

He curled his lip. 'Well, duh. Obviously.'

'Well, duh, Mr Sarcasm.' Martha put her hands on her hips and regarded him pityingly. 'So how come the original animals have been disappearing from the museum, then? It's not as though you need to hide them from the purchasers: no one from Earth's going to turn up here and realise they've been fooled. No one would have suspected anything was going on if it wasn't for that.'

Frank looked slightly sheepish for a second, before covering it up with a defensive sneer. Martha suddenly felt sick. 'Oh, I get it. Quick returns. It was taking too long for the animals to grow up – not enough fur on an infant for a coat, is there? So you started taking the originals.' The sickness turned to anger. 'How could you? Bad enough killing them anyway, but you were committing genocide again and again, for a few quid!' Now the anger turned to contempt. 'Shame you didn't really think it through. You're trying to be a criminal mastermind, but you're obviously just one of those bungling amateur types. So callous you destroyed unique creatures for profit. So incompetent you practically put up a neon sign reading "criminal activity going on here".'

Frank stood up quickly and Martha's first instinct was to step back, thinking he was going to hit her. But she held her ground, and he dropped his raised hand. 'Like you'd understand!' he yelled, causing a dozen dodos to scuttle backwards in alarm. 'Agent Jones, all respected and seven-figure salaried, laying down the law to lesser mortals. How would you know what it's like?'

She almost laughed. When you'd been the only black female in your class, when you had a student loan that could cripple a small country, when you'd endured the sarcasm or shrieking of consultants every time you'd got an answer wrong, when your current idea of stability was to stay in the same time zone for more than an hour…

'Yeah, that's a good excuse,' she said. 'I'd use that when your case comes to trial if I were you.'

His eyes narrowed in hate, and with a shock Martha remembered that she was dealing with someone who was willing to kill. She was catching it from the Doctor – let's mock and patronise the bad guys, because what they can't bear more than anything else is not to be taken seriously. Laughter wasn't only the best medicine; it could also be the best weapon. But the thing to remember about the Doctor was that he was the Doctor. He got away with stuff. And she was still the student, still learning how this all worked.

She'd forgotten that. And Frank had a gun.

Try to calm him down, that was what she had to do. Try to paper over those hasty words, make him forget them. 'Well, why don't you help me to understand, then,' she said. 'You say I don't understand. So tell me why you did it.'

He shrugged. 'Ever been to Kinjana?' Martha shook her head. 'Don't blame you. It's a pit. I knew that when I lived there. Had to get out, and I got a job here. Same body-type as Earth, so that's where I got assigned. I could blend in there. And after a bit, I realised I could. Blend in. I could live there. I could be one of those stinking rich, not a care in the universe. I could wear silk and fur and eat caviar and cream, and be waited on day and night. I'd get women to peel grapes for me, and boys to shine my shoes, and no one would ever tell me what to do. That's what I could have. And if a few stupid animals had to die to give it to me, then, duh – a few stupid animals would die.'

'And a few people too? Tommy's in the infirmary because of you, sliced up by a sabre-toothed tiger, and all so you can have shiny shoes and peeled grapes! And you know what? Most of the nutrients are in the skin, so you'd be the loser there.'

Frank seemed unconcerned. 'Yeah, right, people. Like I care. Even the other Earthers'd agree that *people* don't matter – not next to their precious Last Ones. No one'll blink an eye if I kill you – *when* I kill you, to stop you blabbing. I mean, losing one human don't really matter when there are billions of others still around.' The smile turned into a laugh. 'Well, for now.'

Martha didn't have time to reflect on what he meant by that. She could see nothing but the gun. Nothing but the way it was pointing straight at her. Nothing but the way it shook very slightly as Frank's finger tightened on the trigger…

The door crashed open. 'Frank!' Eve sounded astounded and furious. 'Don't kill her!'

Martha had never been so pleased to see someone she hated. 'Eve!' she cried. 'Frank escaped somehow, he's been cloning these animals and…' She tailed off. Eve was still addressing Frank.

'I don't want her dead, Frank. If she tries to escape you can wound her, but keep her alive.'

Oh.

STELLER'S SEA COW

Hydrodamalis gigas

Location: Commander Islands

This giant sea mammal can reach up to eight metres in length. It has thick grey skin and small, bristly forelimbs.

Addendum:

Last reported sighting: 1768 AD.
Cause of extinction: hunting by man.

I-Spyder points value: 1000

FIFTEEN

Martha had been tied to a chair. It felt vaguely unreal, the sort of thing that happened to heroines in books or silent movies. She should be wearing an enormous frock, and Frank should have a pointed moustache.

And as for Eve…

'You really thought Frank here was behind the cloning?' she said, leafing through a file and not looking at Martha. 'He can't even boil an egg, let alone manipulate DNA.'

Martha tried to shrug, but it didn't quite work. 'Never judge a criminal mastermind book by its cover, that's what I was always taught,' she said. 'You, on the other hand, though – I should have guessed. The murderous tendencies, the callous disregard for life, that top with that skirt…'

'I had to do what I had to do,' Eve said unemotionally. 'The collection was losing money. Subscriptions, entrance fees, a few pounds spent in the gift shop – do you really think that's a drop in the ocean compared to the cost of running this place?'

'So you came up with a plan to make big bucks by selling stuff you couldn't buy in the gift shop. The Last Ones.'

'Don't be ridiculous,' Eve spat. 'I, sell the most precious things in the universe?'

Now Martha got it; just a subtle shift making everything fall in place. 'Oh, right. Cos you're the fanatic. But Frank here…' She turned to where the Earther was looking defiant. 'That was your little sideline, wasn't it? Your own cunning little idea to get a bit of extra cash. You couldn't work the cloning bit, so you took the originals.' Back to Eve. 'Weren't you furious? I'd have been furious. You should have been furious.'

'She was,' Frank said miserably. 'When she had me locked up, I thought she meant it. I thought I was gonna rot in prison.'

'You deserved to,' said Eve. 'And you would have done, if my plans hadn't changed, if I hadn't needed an extra pair of hands again.'

It was at that point that Martha remembered her original mission: to find out what the business with the sabre-tooths and the dodos and the eggs was all about.

'So, this business with the sabre-tooths and the dodos and the eggs – what's that all about, then?' she asked, abandoning any thoughts of subtlety. Her time with the Doctor had led her to discover that villains really did like to tell you all their plans – well, they needed someone to boast to about how clever they were.

'I really don't think it's any of your business,' Eve said.

Oh. Damn. Perhaps it wouldn't be quite that simple.

* * *

On the third sweep down the high street, the Doctor spotted the second dodo, still scrabbling hard in the shop doorway. Reluctantly recalled to the real business of the day, he brought the machine to a halt and said goodbye to Albert. 'You wanna come for a spin round the galaxy?' he'd asked. 'Return the favour.'

But Albert had shaken his head. 'I've got a wife and kids!' he'd said. 'Wouldn't catch me leaving them, no, not if you were offering me the whole universe.'

And the Doctor, who had nobody, had nodded his head and said he understood.

Albert drove off, and the Doctor waved goodbye.

The Time Lord wandered over to the dodo. To his surprise, it appeared to be ticking. The Doctor hadn't encountered very many dodos over the years, but he was fairly certain that, as a rule, they didn't tick.

He got closer. The sound was actually coming from beneath the bird. Yes, there it was – the egg. The round white egg that the dodo had completely failed to bury in the solid pavement. The Doctor leaned down, attempting to sidle his fingers near enough to extract the ovoid, but the bird reacted violently. Its hooked beak might look comical from a distance, but when the sharp point is threatening to skewer your digits to the path, it's no laughing matter.

The Doctor stepped back, and the dodo calmed down – but with an alert look in its eyes that told the Doctor to beware. He considered the situation. It seemed imperative that he examine that egg. On the other hand, having survived an encounter with a load of sabre-toothed tigers, not to mention a dinosaur attack, it would be fairly embarrassing to be mauled by a giant pigeon. If only Martha had still been around – she seemed to have a way with the things…

The Doctor raised a finger in the air. 'Ding!' he said, indicating the metaphorical light bulb that had just lit up above his head. An idea!

He hurried back to the place where Martha had first spotted Dorothea the dodo, and dived into the heap of rubbish that had spilled out of the litter bin. There, nestling in a triangular plastic container that had once contained cheese and pickle sandwiches, was an egg. Or rather, what looked like an egg.

The Doctor picked it up, wiping off a smear of pickle with his sleeve. This one, too, was ticking.

It was a bomb.

The dodos were burying bombs. The Doctor breathed in heavily.

And then, to top it off, another dinosaur attacked him.

'Well, whatever your plans are, the Doctor will stop you,' Martha said.

'Yeah, right,' said Frank, sharing a smirk with Eve.

Martha turned to him. He was manipulating controls at the desk, glancing between them and one of the screens in front of him. She stared. The picture on the screen looked like a dinosaur. Not the one she'd seen briefly before leaving Earth, but one of the smaller ones from the shop's TV screens – not that it really mattered; it still had lots of sharp teeth. And in front of it – a tiny figure, dancing around. A figure in a suit. A figure that might, if you squinted hard enough, appear to be holding a little wand-like device in its hand.

With a desperate effort, she maintained her veneer of calm. 'Eve, if you want to stop one more species becoming extinct, you'd better do something quickly.'

Eve followed Martha's gaze. The dinosaur was bearing down on the Doctor. She ran over to the desk and, pushing Frank aside, dived at the controls. 'You idiot!' she yelled at him. 'The last of the Time Lords! The sole survivor!'

Frank was spluttering in indignation. 'But you told me… If anyone got too close… He'd found one of the bombs, he was going to examine it…'

'And what can he do?!' Eve shouted, still pushing buttons. 'He can't stop us! But if you killed him… He is a Last One! The legacy of an entire planet, destroyed!'

Under other circumstances, Martha would probably have enjoyed seeing Frank squirm. But as it was, she couldn't take her eyes off the screen.

The dinosaur raised a claw, preparing to slash down at the Doctor. And then it seemed to pop out of existence.

An angry roar from behind one of the far doors suggested that the reptile had returned to base. An involuntary sigh of relief hissed out with Martha's exhaled breath. She was still a prisoner. The Last Ones were still stranded on twenty-first-century Earth. But as long as the Doctor was alive and free, she couldn't help but believe that it would turn out all right in the end. Somehow.

And then a word sank in. She realised what Frank had said. '*Bombs?*'

The Doctor stared bemusedly at where the dinosaur had been. Its behaviour had not been what one usually expected of a giant prehistoric carnivorous reptile. Still, compared to the previous one, dealing with it had been a breeze, and he wasn't going to complain about that. He had other things on his mind right now.

He popped the sonic screwdriver back in his pocket and, shrugging, returned his attention to the deadly device in his hand. Holding it gingerly, he walked over to the electricals shop. The news reports still played across a dozen silent screens. China. India. America. Kenya, Iceland, France. Derby, Dundee, Durham. All across the world, there were dodos. All across the world, there were bombs.

The Doctor walked back to the TARDIS. His instinct was to break into a jog, get there quicker, but while one was carrying a bomb... Better safe than sorry. Once into the control room, with the vulnerable world safely on the other side of a pair of impenetrable doors, he whipped out the sonic screwdriver and set to work.

He'd hoped the ticking indicated a timer, something easily disarmed, but the realities of the mechanism made him hiss through his teeth in frustration. There was a timer, yes, but the charge also had a remote-control sensor; someone somewhere had their finger on the trigger and could set off the device at any time they liked, without having to wait for the timer to count down to zero.

How many of these bombs were there throughout the world? He could try to gather them all up, but the trigger finger could tighten at any time – and may well do so if what he was doing was detected. Theoretically, with a time machine he could collect them all at the exact same time – but quite how he'd go about tracking down an unknown number of bombs from an unknown set of locations to start with was another matter altogether. Much, much better to remove the finger from the trigger instead.

And he was fairly certain he knew where the trigger was to be found, and whose hand the finger was part of.

Martha would have sat down in shock if she hadn't already been tied to a chair. Had the Doctor been saved from a dinosaur only to be threatened with something worse?

Eve was glaring at Frank, who was trying to look like he didn't care.

'Bombs?' Martha asked again.

'Oh all right, you might as well know,' Eve said, and began to tell Martha all about her plans, all about the sabre-tooths and the dodos and the eggs.

And after she'd finished, Martha, feeling sick, really wished she'd remained in blissful ignorance.

'You… you can't be serious!' she exclaimed.

'Perfectly,' said Eve.

'But…' Martha couldn't find the words.

Suddenly Eve's cool exterior cracked. 'The pressure,' she hissed. 'The constant pressure. The fear that one day you'll miss one, that a species will slip through your fingers. And Earth – Earth is the worst, by far. Extinction after extinction after extinction, it's a nightmare keeping track! The instant you've updated your records, the stupid humans destroy another rainforest, and there we go again. This way, it will all be over with. I'll never have to worry about it again.'

'But…' The words still weren't coming. 'But… But… you're destroying all life on Earth to *cut down on paperwork*?'

'I'm not destroying all life on Earth,' Eve told her. 'That's exactly the point. I will be going to destroy all life on Earth, and then I will have destroyed all life on Earth. It will happen instantaneously.'

Martha boggled. 'You're committing mass genocide and quibbling about tenses?'

Eve dismissed this with a wave of her hand. 'In a very short time, the clone-dos will have deposited all the bombs, with the clone-tooths and clone-osaurs preventing any interference.'

Martha thought it interesting that the ridiculous names didn't actually defuse the threat at all. In fact, they heightened it, because it made it even clearer that this was the work of a madwoman. But she had spotted a flaw in Eve's plan. 'If you blow up everything, your collection will always be incomplete. You know, because you'll have killed everything.'

This brought a smile to Eve's face. She spoke to Martha as if she were a simpleton who'd overlooked the most obvious of factors. 'But that's the whole point! I admit that I panicked when the disaster first happened, when all the Earth specimens got transported back. But they all died on arrival; the only one of my exhibits that survived for more than a few seconds was a dinosaur. There's not a trace of any of them on Earth any more, the pressure of the return trip must have been too great.'

Martha nearly gagged. She was responsible for the deaths of 300 billion creatures. For wiping out 300 billion species.

She had to switch off again, that was just impossible to deal with.

Eve was still talking. 'But it gave me the idea. A get-out clause! And as long as I have just one specimen to represent the planet – I sent Tommy to collect the dinosaur, but that's gone now too. Thankfully, I have you.'

This was too much. Not only had she sent all those creatures back to Earth, but she'd inspired mass genocide while she was at it. It was all her fault.

And her penance was to be a living death.

'Now if you'll excuse me,' Eve continued, 'I have to see about ordering some new guidebooks. Our current ones will soon be hopelessly out of date.'

'No!' Martha cried. 'Please, you can't do this!' But Eve had already left the room.

KAKAPO

Strigops habroptilus

Location: New Zealand

The kakapo is the world's only flightless parrot. It has an owl-like face and greeny-yellow feathers, with the male being more brightly coloured than the female. They are solitary, each having its own territory, and live on the ground. The herbivorous kakapo is the heaviest known parrot, weighing up to 3.5 kilograms.

Addendum:

Last reported sighting: AD 2017.
Cause of extinction: introduction of non-indigenous predators; hunting for meat and skins.

I-Spyder points value: 900

SIXTEEN

For a few moments, Martha found it hard to breathe. What could she do? She had to do something! But here she was, tied to a chair and helpless. In desperation, she turned to Eve's accomplice, who was still looking slightly sulky after his telling-off. He probably wouldn't care about her, but she could appeal to his self-interest. 'Frank, you've got to stop this! I mean, if you were planning a new life on Earth, why on Earth – no pun intended – did you agree to help her destroy every living thing on the planet? Think of the servants! Think of the grapes!'

He threw up his hands in the air. 'Pay attention! It was that or spend the next however-many-years in prison!'

Martha sighed in disbelief. 'You're strictly a short-term-gain sort of person, aren't you, Frank.' She tried again with a defiance she no longer felt. 'The Doctor will stop you.'

'Yeah, right,' said Frank.

There was a noise like a thousand trumpeting elephants, and the TARDIS appeared.

'Yeah, right!' said Martha, overjoyed.

'Hello,' said the Doctor, bursting through the TARDIS door, his momentum carrying him across the room, plucking Frank's gun out of his hand on the way. A few buzzes from the sonic screwdriver later, the gun was tossed back to Frank, who'd barely had time to realise it had been taken in the first place. In some confusion, Frank gingerly raised the weapon and pointed it at the Doctor, who tutted. 'Franky, Franky, I'm hardly likely to give you back the gun if it still works, am I? Six to one it won't do a thing if you try to shoot, half a dozen of the other it'll explode in your hand. I appear to have mixed up a few expressions in that sentence, but you get the general idea. Shooting equals bad idea.' Scowling, Frank put down the gun.

'I don't like to say "I told you so", Frank…' Martha was laughing with relief as she turned to the Doctor. 'How did you find us?'

The Time Lord whipped a feather out of his pocket. 'Automatic dodo detector!' he said. 'Only I specifically tuned it in to Dorothea this time.' He gave the bird a quick pat on the head. 'What a fantastic invention that is. A million uses.'

'What are the other 999,999?' asked Martha. 'You know, apart from the detecting dodos thing?'

'All right, one use,' the Doctor admitted, leaning over her to untie her bonds. He smelled faintly of peaches and patchouli, and she smiled. 'But you could detect a million different dodos.'

'Like the ones which are burying bombs ready to destroy life on Earth?' Martha said.

'Could do, could do,' said the Doctor, and there was a touch of seriousness underneath his apparent levity. 'But I thought it would be far simpler to deactivate them all at once from the source.'

As he undid the final knot, they heard a door slam. Frank had taken advantage of the Doctor's back being turned to make a getaway.

'He'll have gone to fetch Eve,' Martha said urgently. 'She's the one behind it all!'

'Quelle surprise,' said the Doctor. 'Well, we'd better find the detonator controls soon, then.'

'Yes please,' said Martha. 'Please, please don't let the Earth be destroyed. I don't want to be a Last One.' She smiled weakly. 'Eve's planning to put me in a cage, you know.'

The Doctor froze for a moment, like he was being put in suspended animation again. Was it horror? Or had he had an idea? Martha wasn't sure. She turned her attention back to the immediate problem. 'Frank recalled the dinosaur from over there somewhere,' she said, indicating the desk. 'Perhaps the detonator's in the same place.'

He nodded. 'Good, that means I can bring back the clones while I look.'

'Can't you bring back the bombs too?' Martha asked.

The nod switched to a shake. 'They'll have been buried by now, they're no longer in contact with the dodo carriers.' The Doctor began to search frantically, sorting through piles of equipment with one hand while tapping on the computer keypad with the other. Martha hurried round the rest of the room, looking for anything that looked at all technological and remote-detonator-like.

After a few minutes, the Doctor took a step back and ran his fingers through his hair. 'Nothing!' he said, a touch of panic shading his voice. 'I've sorted the dinosaurs – dromaeosaurs, I think, it means "fast-running lizard", I suppose she couldn't get away with breeding anything much bigger, and – sorry, getting distracted, matter in hand, matter in hand, yes, sorted them and the sabre-tooths and the dodos, but not the faintest tiny smidgen of a trace of a remote detonator.'

'Look again, you might have missed it!' said Martha, who had climbed into the dodo pen and was now crawling around on hands and knees, just in case the controls had been hidden on the floor there.

'I don't miss things,' said the Doctor. 'Well, not that sort of thing. Birthdays, I'm terrible with. Socks! I'm always losing socks. Never have enough socks. If you're ever trying to think what to get me for Christmas, socks is what I'd suggest. Remote bomb activation controls, on the other hand, I'm good with. If they're there, I find them.'

The door opened and Eve walked in. The Doctor sprang towards her. 'Eve! You mustn't do this!'

She smiled at him. 'But that's just it. I *must*.'

He shook his head. 'No-no-no-no-no!'

Eve continued to smile as the Doctor turned to the work bench, flinging circuit boards and test tubes over his shoulders as he searched and discarded. 'Where are the controls?' he yelled at her furiously.

'Oh, they're near at hand,' she told him. 'But you'll never find them. Don't waste your energy. And if you try anything, I'll just detonate the bombs remotely anyway.'

'I don't think so,' the Doctor said – and he pulled a white sphere from his pocket. It was ticking quietly.

Martha yelped. 'Is that…?'

'Uh-huh. If Eve doesn't deactivate the bombs, bang goes her museum. Well, part of it.'

'The part with us in,' Martha felt she had to point out.

The ticking got suddenly louder. Much louder.

'What's that?'

'Countdown,' replied the Doctor, grimly. 'We've got, ooh, maybe five minutes before all the bombs explode.'

Martha stared. 'Five minutes. Until the end of the Earth.'

'Unless Eve intervenes, yes.'

Eve and the Doctor had locked eyes. 'You're bluffing,' she said. 'You've disconnected the charge.'

'Want to bet on it?' he replied, not smiling.

'You wouldn't destroy her. You wouldn't risk other people's lives.'

'To save a whole planet? I think I might.'

Eve shrugged, but her gaze remained fixed. 'I leave the room. I lock you in. I teleport back to my office. We're not near enough the exhibits to damage them. Everything else in here is a clone. I'm not going to deactivate the bombs.'

'You're bluffing!' Martha said suddenly. 'You don't want the Doctor dead. Or me, come to that. He's a Last One, I'm a Last-One-to-be. You must be bluffing.'

Eve didn't smile. 'Want to bet on it?'

The Doctor blinked first. He turned away and sighed, as the bomb ticked on, measuring out Earth's last seconds.

Dodos clustered around Martha's ankles as she stood in the pen, waiting for the Doctor's next move. But suddenly she saw a look in his eyes that she'd never had a glimpse of before. A look of defeat. But – they still had minutes! Whole minutes before life on Earth was wiped out! Everything she'd discovered about the Doctor so far had led her to believe that that was plenty of time for him to save the day. In fact, he preferred to leave it that late…

Surely he hadn't given up now?

'I think you will deactivate them,' the Doctor said to Eve, and Martha breathed a sigh of relief. He had a plan!

But in that case, why was he still looking so defeated?

'I don't think I will,' Eve replied.

'But I've got a bargain to offer you.' The Doctor took a deep breath. 'If you agree not to destroy the Earth – you can have me.'

'What?' yelled Martha, horror-struck.

The Doctor didn't look at her, kept his gaze fixed on Eve. 'I'll voluntarily become an exhibit. The last of the Time Lords. The most elusive specimen in the universe. Only survivor of an extinct world. The One Cent Magenta. I'll do that, if you disable your bombs. Don't destroy the Earth. And then you won't have to imprison Martha, either. She can go home.'

For a moment, Eve was clearly tempted. But Martha could see the madness rising in her eyes.

'I need Martha,' she said. 'I need both of you. But I have to destroy everything else. Do you know what I felt?' she said, a beatific smile spreading across her face. 'Do you know what I felt when I made the decision about Earth? I felt relief.'

The Doctor took a step towards her, but she waved him back. 'One more step, and *boom!*' she said. She sighed. 'I've been doing this for ever. And I thought my job would never end, not until the end of the universe itself. But this forced me to think about it – and I found a loophole.'

'It's all about tenses, apparently,' Martha said, resisting the temptation to make a 'she's screwy!' gesture.

The Doctor looked interested. 'Really?' He looked at Eve. 'Care to explain?'

She said, as if it made perfect sense, 'I have to stop any species from dying out. And I have to make sure every planet is represented, remembered somehow. But this way, with the bombs – there is no point at which any species is dying out, just a single specimen remaining. Each species is fine – and then it has died out…'

'You what?' said the Doctor. 'I think you could do with a dictionary, this whole dying, dying out business. Martha, if you're ever stuck on what to buy Eve for Christmas, a dictionary's probably an idea.'

'Christmas?' said Eve, happy again. 'There won't be any more Christmas. You see, I've realised that I needn't stop at Earth. If I have to carry on until the universe ends, then I'll end the universe. As long as I have one specimen from each planet, I'll finally have peace! I'll finally have… *closure*, I think they call it. I'll have closure.'

'Most people try therapy first,' the Doctor said. 'Destroying the universe tends to be a last resort.'

Martha shut her eyes. Time was ticking on – like the bomb – and Eve seemed lost in some strange incomprehensible non-logic of her own. She couldn't see a way that this could end well.

But the Doctor was speaking again. 'I hate to have to break it to you, Eve – but you're never going to manage it. You keep talking about the universe like it's something quantifiable, but it isn't, not really. You're talking about the bit of the universe known to you. Look at Earth – that's just one planet in one solar system. There are maybe, ooh, 50 billion planets in the Milky Way galaxy alone, and that's just one of a few trillion galaxies, in a universe that keeps expanding. I've seen the list of planets in your lobby – you've been looking at the Milky Way, maybe a bit of Andromeda – but where are Beaus, M82, M83, M84, Celation, Isop, Kinrexian? It would take you billions of years to destroy all life in the universe, even if you were capable of it – and by the time you'd got to the last planet, got your last single specimen, life would have sprung up again on the first ones – it can be amazingly resilient. Face it, Eve – you're never going to achieve peace that way.'

Eve staggered backwards. 'All for nothing. It's all been for nothing. I have failed in my objective. I cannot complete my mission.'

'Oh well, missions aren't everything—' the Doctor began, but Eve screamed at him to shut up. She had sat down at the desk, and her eyelids were blinking at an alarming rate.

'So… so… I don't need either of you after all.' She picked up Frank's gun from the desk and pointed it towards them.

'Don't!' yelled the Doctor and Martha together – but Eve had already pulled the trigger.

The gun exploded backwards. Eve slumped heavily to the floor.

Martha took a running jump, scattering dodos to all sides, and leapt over the pen wall. But as she reached the fallen body, she slowed down. There was no blood. Instead…

'She's an android!'

The Doctor joined her, gazing down at the smoking hole where Eve's chest had been. Wires sparked and fizzed.

'I did wonder,' he said. 'All that odd logic. Her not being affected by the psychic paper. And she seemed to have been around for a very long time.'

The ticking from the bomb suddenly increased in speed and pitch. 'Talking of very long times,' he added, 'that's exactly what we don't have.'

'We've got to find those controls!' Martha stared around her in panic. 'They might not even be in this room!'

'No, Eve said they were close at hand...' The Doctor had his fingers to his forehead. 'Think, Doctor, think!' He span on the spot. 'Close at hand! And she's an android...' He threw himself onto his knees beside the motionless Eve and grabbed her wrist, as if feeling for a pulse. The bleeping from the bomb was getting louder and louder, faster and faster, till it was an almost continuous shriek. The whirr of the sonic screwdriver provided an electronic counterpoint as the Doctor wielded it, and Martha couldn't help wincing as he appeared to unscrew one of Eve's fingers. Her gaze darted between these operations and the screens showing scenes on Earth, expecting any second for the views to flare out of existence as she herself stopped existing too...

But they didn't. And she didn't. And the noises stopped, from both bomb and screwdriver.

The Doctor was sitting up, waving a disconnected finger in the air in triumph.

Martha heaved a very big sigh of relief.

* * *

The adrenalin had been rushing around so much that, when it seeped away, I could have fallen asleep there and then on the floor of the secret laboratory. I had a real 'end of story' feel, a real 'happily ever after' – until I realised that it hadn't and it wouldn't be, because there were so many loose ends left that the whole event-pullover might easily unravel. Frank was still running about somewhere; I didn't know what had happened to Tommy; and we might have to explain to people why the museum curator was currently unavailable.

'I thought we'd had it then,' I said.

'Oh, there was plenty of time to chuck this one into an isolation field inside the TARDIS if it came to it,' the Doctor said and tossed the egg-bomb onto the workbench. I yelped, couldn't help it, even though I knew it was OK now, but the thing just rolled harmlessly along until it came to rest against a Bunsen burner. It might have been nice if he'd told me I wasn't about to die – but then I remembered what had led up to this point, and realised that I'd deserved that terror. Because there was the thing, the big thing, the thing that knocked the 'happily' out of 'ever after' for good – the billions of creatures whose deaths I'd caused. The Last Ones. Genocide on a scale that was frankly incomprehensible. Now I didn't have anything else to concentrate on, it threatened to overwhelm me.

I tried to tell the Doctor, who was now engaged in playing tug of war with Dorothea – she seemed to have taken a fancy to some of the wires poking out of Eve's chest, presumably thinking they were skinny worms. But he didn't let me get half of it out before he jumped up from the floor shouting:

'My plan! I nearly forgot!' He bounded towards the door, so I bundled up Dorothea and headed after him.

'Where are we off to?' I said.

'Central computer. Eve's office.'

'Why?'

'Because I –' he tapped his chest importantly as he ran – 'came up with the most stupendous plan that will sort out everything!'

'But Eve said all the animals were dead…'

'Not if I have anything to do with it.'

'So what's the plan?' I asked eagerly.

'No time, no time!' the Doctor cried, racing ahead.

But it didn't really matter to me that I didn't know the details. The adrenalin was surging again. The animals weren't dead – and everything was going to be all right.

PARADISE PARROT

Psephotus pulcherrimus

Location: Australia

The male of the beautiful paradise parrot,
a native of north-eastern Australia, can be
recognised by its distinctive blue-green
plumage, with striking black and red wings,
tail and cap. The female's feathers are duller,
although still attractive. Its diet consists mainly
of grass seeds.

Addendum:

Last reported sighting: AD 1927.
Cause of extinction: competition for food from
alien livestock; demands of the pet trade

I-Spyder points value: 500

SEVENTEEN

So all I knew about the plan was that it involved the central computer in Eve's office. But then, even if the Doctor explained, I'd probably have been none the wiser. I mean, I can set the DVD recorder, wire a plug and have even been known to fix the toaster, but the sort of technology we were talking about here was a little bit beyond me.

Don't ask me how the Doctor knew the way from the secret lab to Eve's office – he's that sort of person. I wonder if Time Lords have a bit of homing pigeon in their ancestry too. Anyway, we reached it in super-quick time and the Doctor dashed inside, only to find Rix, Nadya, Vanni and Celia already there. They all looked a bit worried, which was perfectly reasonable.

'Doctor!' Vanni said (people do that, you know. It's always 'Doctor!' Never 'Martha!' Same with villains. 'Get the Doctor and the girl!' Oh well, maybe one day it'll be 'Get Martha and the man!' and he'll know what it feels like to be the anonymous spare part. Not that I actually want to be captured by villains or anything, I should point out). 'Do you know what's going on?' Vanni continued.

'All the traces disappeared from Earth,' Nadya said. 'Goodness knows what sort of mess there is down there…'

'So we came to find Eve, but she's not here,' added Celia.

'Tommy's in the infirmary, but no one knows how he was hurt,' said Rix.

'And Celia went to see Frank in detention but he wasn't there,' Vanni finished.

I stood there, trying to think how to explain it all to them in ways that would not get me into a lot of trouble, but the Doctor got there first. 'To take your points in reverse order,' he said, 'Frank's on the loose somewhere, sabre-toothed tiger, Eve's indisposed—'

'And an android,' I put in helpfully.

'—and I'm here to clean up the mess for you.' He sat down at Eve's computer and started to tap away. I envy that. Put him in front of any futuristic machine and he's there straight away, he doesn't even have to search for the on switch.

'An android?' said Celia, as this interesting and probably rather surprising fact seemed to finally penetrate. 'What do you mean, an android?'

The Doctor didn't look up from the screen. 'Looks like another candidate for a dictionary. Android: humanoid automaton. Martha, you could give that dictionary you were going to buy for Eve to Celia instead, seeing as Eve won't be needing it, what with being a humanoid automaton an' all.'

Celia got all huffy at that, not that I entirely blamed her, so I did my best to explain to her and the other Earthers what it was all about. Not that that amounted to much more than 'we know she's an android because when her chest exploded it was full of wires and no, she probably won't be back at work for a while'.

Just as I was stumbling to the end of my inadequate explanation, the Doctor turned away from the computer in frustration. 'Bother,' he said.

'What is it?' I asked.

'Password protected.' He looked at the Earthers. 'Anyone know Eve's password?'

They shook their heads. 'Bother,' he said again.

It didn't seem like that big a deal to me. 'Surely you can work it out,' I said.

He looked at me pityingly. 'It was set up by an android who has an android's sophisticated electronic brain. She won't have used the name of her first pet or her favourite TV character, it'll be some immensely complex and unguessable formula of hundreds of symbols. It'll take hours, days even, to work out.'

Needless to say, I felt crushed. 'Would Frank know it?' I suggested, trying to make amends for my stupidity. 'He's obviously been working closely with Eve.'

He grimaced. 'Maybe. But Frank's bound to have made his escape by now. He'll have found out that his protectress has gone all explody, and got off planet before anyone decides to tick him off for all the attempted genocide.'

I felt crushed again. But Vanni said, 'How? There aren't any tourist ships due for hours.'

'And he can't teleport off,' put in Rix. 'He'd need to get his pendant back off Tommy first.'

We all looked at each other. 'Tommy!'

We were all set to race out of the door, but Nadya waved a hand to stop us. 'It's all right,' she said, 'Frank won't know where to find him. Why would he think of looking in the infirmary?'

Ah. 'Um…' I said, trying to run through my most recent conversations with Frank in my head. Surely I hadn't mentioned it. Or had I? Oh bum, I was fairly sure I had…

'Martha?' said the Doctor.

'Sorry,' I replied, answering the implication.

We all raced out of the door.

Martha headed the charge from Eve's office until she realised she had no idea where the infirmary was and therefore fell back to let Rix lead. The others would probably have overtaken her anyway; she was still carrying Dorothea and so speed was not currently her strong point. She wished she hadn't abandoned the shopping trolley earlier.

What this all meant, though, was that she reached the infirmary a few seconds after the others, and so she was the last to see that they were already too late.

Tommy was lying in a bed, conscious, and hooked up to monitors that were giving out reassuring beeping sounds. These were all good things. What was not good at all, however, was that standing over the recumbent man was Frank, a determined look on his face. There was a great big holdall at the ex-Earther's feet, bundles of notes sticking out of the top. His ill-gotten gains.

'Tommy!' shouted Rix, making to rush forwards, but Frank yelled 'Stop!' He'd got a new gun from somewhere, and it now swivelled round to point at Rix.

'Glad you could join us. Tommy doesn't want to tell me where my pendant is, however much I promise to hurt him. But I reckon he might have second thoughts if I promise to kill all you lot instead.' Nadya's hand had been creeping towards her own pendant, but she suddenly screamed as a laser beam shot past her neck, exploding a vase of flowers on a cabinet behind her. 'Don't do that, Nadya,' Frank continued, as chrysanthemum petals rained down on the ward. 'In fact, it'd be a good plan if you all took off your pendants and threw them over here. And if I see any fingers near buttons, then I shoot, and it won't be a warning shot.'

The Earthers unhappily did as he instructed, tossing their pendants at Frank's feet. The gun never wavering, he bent down and gathered them up, pushing them in his pocket. 'Now, Tommy...?' he said as he straightened up again.

'You killed them! The quagga, the bluebuck, everything! And you expect me to help you escape?' growled Tommy from the bed.

'Duh!' said Frank. 'I've just been explaining that. Because if you don't, I'll kill all your friends here, one by one.'

'I'm more a sort of acquaintance, actually,' put in the Doctor. 'No offence, Tommy.'

Frank sighed. 'All right, all your friends *and acquaintances* here.'

'And, not that I'm really the one to judge or cast aspersions on anyone's relationships, but the thing about work is that you get flung together with people out of necessity rather than choice, so I wonder if some of the people here would be better described merely as colleagues rather than friends...'

'Fine. All your friends and acquaintances *and colleagues* here.'

The Doctor nodded. Then stopped. 'Hang on, hang on, my fault, but when you come to think of it, friends and colleagues are by necessity acquaintances too. So really, you could just say "acquaintances" and that covers the lot. Save some time.'

Frank gritted his teeth. 'Shut up!'

'Righteo.' There was a pause, then the Doctor added, 'Wait a mo, I've forgotten what it was you were going to do to the friends and acquaintances and colleagues in the first place.'

'I was going to kill them!' yelled Frank.

'Ah, yes, that was it. Knew it was something like that.'

Martha couldn't help smiling, despite yet another threat of imminent death. The Doctor really did have a Grade A in Annoying.

But maybe this was her chance: on with the nasty cop, nice cop routine. Or rather, irritating cop, reasonable cop. She put down Dorothea and walked towards Frank with her hands outstretched to show she was no threat. 'Frank, I reckon we can work this all out,' she began, but before she could continue Frank had grabbed hold of her extended arm and yanked her towards him. The Doctor started forwards but stopped hurriedly as Frank jammed the pistol against Martha's ear.

He smiled. 'Tommy, tell me where my pendant is, or Martha loses her head.'

'Frank, no!' cried Celia.

'Didn't know you cared,' Martha muttered. But if Celia

could persuade Frank to put down the gun, then Celia was her new best friend and no mistake.

'You don't want to do this, Frank. You're a good man, really, I know that. You just… lost your way.'

'Sheesh, Ceel, and I was just getting used to the idea of never hearing your moaning voice again,' said Frank, dashing Martha's hopes. 'After Martha, you're next. Hey, I may even shoot you first, just to make sure of a bit of peace and quiet.'

Whimpering, Celia retreated. Frank waggled the gun and raised his eyebrows questioningly at Tommy. 'Well?'

'Just tell him, Tom!' called Nadya. 'The authorities will pick him up anyway.'

Scowling, Tommy nodded. He reached across to a drawer in the bedside cabinet, opened it, and pulled out a pendant.

Frank's face showed a mixture of triumph and annoyance. 'You mean it was there all the time?'

Tommy shrugged, holding out the teleport device. 'Drawer wasn't even locked.'

Frank took the pendant, maintaining a stranglehold on Martha while he examined it closely, then he nodded and hung it around his neck. One-handed, he began to programme it with coordinates.

Martha tensed as the final digit was inputted. Surely he'd just zap away now, make his getaway… But he didn't. Instead, Frank put his free hand into a pocket and pulled out a small white sphere.

'That's a bomb!' she gasped.

'Well, duh,' said Frank. 'Funny thing, there's me thinking all the bombs had gone off to Earth, but what do I find when

I get back to the lab? Earth still lousy with life, RIP Eve – and a bomb on the bench. Thought it might come in handy. Cos Nadya had a point there, thanks, Nard. The authorities might be after me. But not if there's no one left to tell 'em about it. I just need to destroy the evidence. And you're the evidence.'

'You mean "witnesses",' said the Doctor. 'Sounds like you could do with one of the Christmas dictionaries that were on offer earlier. But I wouldn't get your hopes up. I reckon you're going on Santa's "naughty" list for, ooh, ever.'

But Frank wasn't letting the Doctor get to him any more. 'Fine, witnesses,' he said. 'Call yourselves what you want, you'll be just as dead – and in so many pieces they'll never work out how many bodies there are. And then I'll be safely away with my servants and my grapes, right, Martha?' He rubbed the gun against her neck. Martha didn't say anything. She couldn't take her eyes off the egg-bomb, as Frank primed the mechanism. It began to tick in time with the bleepings from Tommy's monitors.

Bending down carefully, the gun still pointed at Martha, Frank placed the bomb on the floor. 'Enjoy your last thirty seconds,' he said, and his hand reached for his pendant…

And so did Martha's hand. 'You enjoy it too, Frank,' she said, yanking the pendant so hard the cord snapped. She flung the device to the Doctor and, as Frank yelled in pain, she knocked the gun out of his hand. He pushed her aside and she fell to the floor, but grabbed hold of his ankles as she did so, pulling him down too. 'Quick, the other pendants!' she yelled, and the Doctor, already on the move towards them, understood at once. He tried to grab at Frank's overalls – but

Frank had retrieved the gun, and an energy beam narrowly missed the Doctor's head.

Martha froze as the pistol swivelled between her and the Doctor, both now lying on the floor. 'I'm sorry,' she whispered. 'I was going to try to get away with the bomb.'

'Yeah, I'm sorry too,' said Frank, hurrying over to pick up his pendant. 'Sorry to spoil your oh-so-heroic self-sacrifice. But you know what? You've inspired me. I'm not going to let you all die. I'm going to devote my life to good works.' But Martha wasn't listening. From her prone position on the floor she had seen something.

Dorothea.

The dodo had recognised the white sphere that Frank had rested on the floor. In among all the unfamiliarity, this was something she knew. The dodos had gone over this again and again with Frank. He gave them an egg, and they were supposed to bury it. It seemed to her that Frank had once again given her an egg. So she should bury it.

But for a shattered vase of flowers, the infirmary room was stark and gleaming. There was a bed, a cabinet, a trolley holding equipment, and some monitors. Nothing that she could reach, nothing suitable for a burial.

But there was a bag. It was on the floor, and it was full of papery stuff, just perfect for covering up an egg. She waddled over to the egg and started to push it along with her claws, towards the bag.

With considerable effort, she used her great beak to nudge the egg the few inches up the side of the bag until it plopped softly into its paper nest. A few sweeps with the tip of her beak and it was fully concealed.

I'll give all my wodges of cash to the poor…' Frank was continuing. Then he laughed. 'Yeah, right!' He picked up his bag of money. 'Seven – six – five –' He pressed the blue button on his pendant – and vanished.

'Four… three… two… one,' said the Doctor.

There was a stunned silence as the Earthers, who had all been holding their breath, suddenly realised they were still alive and could let it out again. A grinning Martha started to explain, but as they caught on whoops and cries and laughs of relief drowned her out. Nadya hugged Rix, and Vanni hugged the Doctor, and Tommy managed to pull himself to a sitting position in bed and punched the air. Martha grabbed Dorothea and the two of them did an ungainly waltz around the room. Celia cheered the loudest of all – well, thought Martha, it's like a messy divorce; it's going to be the ex-partner who's happiest when someone blows themselves to smithereens.

'Oh!' said Vanni suddenly, 'I hope he doesn't materialise anywhere where there are people…'

The laughter stopped, but Martha kept dancing. 'Nope,' she said. 'He's gone to that warehouse on Earth. I recognised the coordinates.' And then she realised something too and stumbled to a halt. 'But we never got Eve's password from him!' She turned to the Doctor in dismay.

'What do you need Eve's password for?' Tommy asked.

'All those animals on Earth,' Martha told him. 'The ones that got… accidentally transported there.'

'What about them?'

'I'm going to return them all,' said the Doctor. 'Once I get into the central computer.'

The Earthers all looked delighted, and Tommy nodded. 'Oh, right. Lucky I have access as head of the Earth team. The password's "Hr'oln". H, r, apostrophe, o, l, n. Eve's first pet, apparently.'

The Doctor looked very slightly sheepish.

GREAT AUK

Pinguinus impennis

Location: North Atlantic

The Great Auk is a flightless bird that resembles a penguin. It lives in the sea but comes ashore on islands to breed. It has a black back and head with a white underbelly, and white patches above its large, slightly hooked beak.

Addendum:

Last reported sighting: AD 1844.
Cause of extinction: hunting by man.

I-Spyder points value: 800

EIGHTEEN

The medical computers reported that Tommy was well enough to leave the infirmary, but I couldn't bring myself to entirely trust non-sentient doctors, so I insisted on giving him a thorough check-up first. But it only confirmed the computers' verdict, so I wagged my finger and told him to be more careful in future, and then let him get up. The Doctor had already dashed off to Eve's office; Tommy suggested we all meet up in the Earth section afterwards. So the remaining six of us – seven, if you included Dorothea – trooped off and waited for him by the empty dodo case. It seemed rather appropriate.

We'd been standing there for a few minutes when I spotted the Doctor approaching. Well, there wasn't anything to mask his approach. As far as the eye could see, the Earth section was still absolutely empty.

'You couldn't do it?' I asked him, trying to keep the dismay out of my voice.

'Yes, I could,' he replied.

Everyone looked puzzled, and I'm sure I did too. 'So… it didn't work,' Rix said.

'Oh, I think it did.' The Doctor appeared rather pleased with himself. 'Thing is, when I said I was returning everything, I didn't actually mean I was bringing them back here. They've all gone home. When you've got a time machine in the mix…'

'You sent them back to their own times!' I exclaimed. Then I realised what that meant. 'To die alone…' I hugged Dorothea.

But the Doctor was still smiling. 'Well, I may not have got it spot on,' he said. 'You know, tricky to get these things exact. It's entirely possible that they may have arrived quite a few years before they left, when members of their species were plentiful.'

I gaped at him. Wasn't that the sort of thing people were warned about, in science-fiction stories and stuff? 'But… couldn't they end up being their own grandparents or something?'

He shrugged. 'Maybe. I don't think it'll worry them that much. No one's going to get out the family photo album and say, "Hey – that jellyfish looks familiar."'

And then I thought about how Eve had been willing to freeze the Doctor and me. 'But there might have been, you know, people.'

He looked suddenly serious. 'Then I hope they'll forgive me.'

I thought about it for a second, about how I'd feel if it were me. But I couldn't imagine it.

'So… sort of a happy ending,' I said, but I couldn't feel

completely happy inside. I knew that not every animal would have got back home. Because of me.

'Which ones were those?' the Doctor asked, but the guilt was hitting too hard for me to spot the twinkle in his eye.

'You know – the ones that landed in the sea and stuff on modern Earth.'

'Ah, yes.' Now I couldn't fail to notice that he looked happier than events warranted. 'While you were down on Earth – did you notice a single dinosaur apart from that Megalosaurus?'

'Er, yes,' I said. 'They were the big ones with teeth on the TV, weren't they?'

'Ah, not the dromaeosaurs, they were clones,' he said. 'Like the sabre-toothed tigers and the dodos. Funny thing, when I came to think about it – the news reports, TV, all over the world – not a sign of anything other than those three species, which was a bit odd, considering that 300 billion creatures should have just materialised. In fact, the only non-clone seemed to be the Megalosaurus, which, funnily enough, was the one that gave me the idea in the first place.'

I was possibly not following this quite as well as I'd have liked. 'Come again?' I said. 'Words of one syllable might be a good idea. How come the animals weren't there? I sent them all back.'

He grinned. 'You did. And I hijacked them all on arrival.'

'So not only did you send them back to a time before they were collected…

'I picked them up a few hours before I'd had the idea of doing it in the first place. Them and any strays left over from

Frank's business empire. Little Mervin the missing link, for example.'

'So what about the Megalosaurus?'

'Well, I knew I had to make an exception for it, because without it the pendant would never have had anything to track back to twenty-first-century Earth, so I'd never have met it, and I'd never have had the idea to send the animals back to before their own times which I had to exclude it from.'

Sometimes, listening to the Doctor, you got the impression that someone had taken a perfectly sensible, straightforward thought and then cut and pasted it at random all over the place. I just nodded and went 'mm'. The others did too.

For a moment, everyone just stood around going 'mm'. Then Nadya said, 'You know what this means? We're all out of a job.'

'Probably get a transfer to another section…' said Vanni.

'Ah.' That was the Doctor, in his 'spanner in the works' voice. 'When I said I was returning everything – I really did mean everything. Seemed a waste, being in the central computer for the whole museum and not taking advantage of it… There are no more sections. There are no more exhibits.'

'No more MOTLO?'

'Nail on the head, that girl.'

The Earthers all looked a bit lost. Cancel that, a lot lost. 'So… what happens now?' asked Celia. 'Things will still be going extinct.'

I nodded. 'Yeah,' I said. I had a thought. 'But it's OK to

feel passionate about it. Like how you attacked the poacher who was trying to shoot the rhino? Why not try to stop the extinctions in a different sort of way?'

She sniffed, and I suppose that had been a bit patronising of me. But I'd noticed a spark in her eyes while I was speaking, and I think it might have hit home. Perhaps for all of them.

And you'd think that would be it. The end of the story. Goodbyes said, and loose ends all wrapped up. Eve and Frank defeated! The Earth saved! The animals returned home! Back to the TARDIS for tea and crumpets and on our way to another adventure.

But it wasn't. There was more to come. And quite a surprising more it was too.

The Doctor and Martha headed back to the TARDIS. 'Oh,' said Martha as they arrived in the relevant corridor. 'Um… I don't actually know how to open the secret door from this side. Frank sort of let me in the first time.'

'And I didn't use the door at all,' said the Doctor. He pulled the sonic screwdriver out of his pocket. 'Luckily I have a key that fits any lock…'

The screwdriver hummed, and to Martha's relief the secret door clicked open.

And so did the other secret door.

It was on the opposite side of the corridor, and led into a very small, spartan room. Inside was a clear case, the same as all the other ones in the museum – and there was one single, solitary exhibit frozen inside.

Martha frowned. 'I thought you sent everything back,' she said to the Doctor.

He was frowning as well. 'I thought I did too.' He took a couple of steps closer, and his eyes widened in recognition. 'Do you realise what this is?' he asked Martha.

She shook her head. 'Should I?'

He pulled the pendant out of his pocket and held it up, displaying the MOTLO logo. A line drawing of a creature's head, a creature with tusks and triangular eyes.

Martha took the pendant and edged nearer, peering intently at the head of the creature inside the case. 'It's the same thing,' she said. 'Except… this one looks like it's crying. There's a tear on its cheek.'

There was a label, not a neat computer-generated one like the other exhibits had had, but small and handwritten. Martha bent down to read it. '"Hr'oln",' she said. 'Hang on, h, r, apostrophe, o, l, n. That was Eve's password. Her first pet, Tommy said.' She looked again at the animal. It reminded her a bit of the Steller's sea cow she'd seen in the museum, although only a quarter of the size of that giant animal and with arms instead of flippers. 'Not exactly a cat or dog.'

'I think,' the Doctor told her, 'that it's Eve's very first "specimen", the thing she built the museum around. If it was never *collected* in the first place, my watchamadoodles with the computer wouldn't have affected it. But that doesn't mean I can't get it home.'

He took out the sonic screwdriver and used it to switch off the stasis field.

The tusked head slowly lifted and, after 500 million years, the tear fell. The creature opened its mouth. 'Eve?' it said.

ANKYLOSAURUS

Ankylosaurus magniventris

Location: North America

The herbivorous Ankylosaurus walks on four legs. It is about five metres long and 1.5 metres high. It is extensively covered with bone, including bone plates on its back and head and bone spikes on its tail and legs, and has a distinctive club at the end of its tail, also made out of bone.

Addendum:

Last reported sighting: late Cretaceous period. Cause of extinction: environmental changes.

I-Spyder points value: 650

NINETEEN

My name is Hr'oln, and I am the last of the Cirranins. The Doctor has persuaded me that it is important to write down my story. He himself appears in the story, although not until the end – but I do not think that is the reason he wants it told. I believe the Doctor has been in many, many stories, and has no particular need to be recognised through one more.

No, I think he wants me to tell my story as an act of remembrance for my people. It is a thing that I must do, but not yet. It may have been hundreds of millions of years but, for me, the pain is still raw. So for now I will just explain how I got to be here.

I am – was – a scientist, back on my home planet. We were a technologically advanced people, which proved to be our undoing. There was a terrible, final war. The whole planet was destroyed and everything on it – every Cirranin, every Vish, every Elipig, every Grun. But… there was me.

I was a pioneer, I had flown to the stars. I had been

expecting a hero's welcome when I returned home. But there was no home to return to.

Grief-stricken, I flew on. My shuttle was still experimental, not built for long distances but, just as it began to fail, I found a new world. This world. It was not all I had hoped for – the people were few, and they were primitive. My appearance scared them, so I constructed an android in their image to interact, and named it Eve. I gave it all my technical knowledge, equipped it with circuits that would allow it to develop and grow and build on what I had taught it. Between us, we began work on a teleportation system that would allow me to visit other planets, perhaps find others closer to my own kind – although the loss of my people was a wound that would never heal.

And then disaster hit this planet too. Not, this time, through manufactured annihilation, but through nature's curse: plague.

Medicine was not my field, but I thought that there might be a cure out there, somewhere. I began work on a process of suspending life functions, of keeping a living being in a state of continued existence. In this way, they could be preserved until the solution was found.

I was too late. On the day I completed the process, the last native died.

My alien physiology may not have been affected by the disease, but my heart began to burst.

Up to that point, the people of this planet had meant little to me, but I realised then that they meant everything. With my teleport not yet complete, they were the only living beings I knew. Eve was my constant companion, and I had designed her – by that time I thought of her as 'her' – to be indistinguishable from an animate individual, but she was in reality nothing more than a construction. After losing my own people, I could not bear the idea that another species was gone for ever. The thoughts that I had been trying to contain erupted inside me. The universe would never know another Elipig. The Grun would fade into myth and legend – if that. Generations of children would grow up on a million worlds, but not one of them would ever stroke a pet Fruzin or take it for a walk. And now this race, too, was lost.

I cried for three days.

Then I said to Eve: We must stop any more species dying out.

She said to me: How do you know when a species is dying out?

And I suddenly thought: *My* species is dying out. I had thought of it as dead, but it isn't, not yet. I said this to her, I said that I was the only one left and when I was gone my people would be no more. I see now that she took me at my word. In her eyes, a species was dying out if and only if there was only one example left. I should have talked to her about conservation, education, helping a species to continue. But I didn't.

I told her that these species mustn't be lost. That the rest of the universe must know about them. Every one must be preserved. Every planet must be remembered.

And she said to me: I understand. Your species is dying out. It must not be lost. It must be preserved. Your planet must be remembered.

I didn't realise what she meant, not until it was too late.

And as I realised, I shed a tear for my people, who had no future, and that is all I knew for millions of years.

Then the Doctor came into my story. He was there when I awoke, although to me it did not seem that I had slept, just that I blinked and the world changed. The news was broken to me of where and when I was, of what Eve had done at my unwitting behest. You would think a person could not take it in, 500 million years passing in an instant, but when you have already lost the planet you knew, to lose the universe you knew seems barely a step further on.

But… it did not have to remain lost. The Doctor made me an offer: he could send me back to my own world, before it was destroyed. My heart sang. To be with my own people again!

But I could not change history, he told me. I could not prevent the planet's destruction, I could not warn my people.

I said to him: if this were you, would you do it? He looked sad for a moment, and then told me it had to be my decision.

And though I had thought I would trade everything for another glimpse of a Kivurd or Fuffox, I realised that I couldn't do it. How could I live every day, knowing what was going to happen yet being unable to stop it? I would stay here, and try to make up, in some small measure, for what my creation had done.

Eve's collection was no more, the Doctor told me, and although I knew why he had done what he had done, my heart felt hollow for all those species condemned to non-existence. I told the Doctor, and he smiled. There were DNA samples, he said. There was Eve's cloning apparatus. And there was a whole planet going spare.

I do not know if I can learn the skills required in the time I have left. I will rebuild Eve, and give her a new task. But this time, I will be careful. This time, things will be different.

So here I am. The last of the Cirranins. When I am gone, my people will be no more. The Doctor has other stories to go on to, but mine approaches its end. So I will, soon, do as the Doctor suggests and tell my tale, and then the Cirranins will live on, in a way. Perhaps, even, my own DNA… Well, I shall think on it.

I thought Hr'oln was going to cry again when we took her into the laboratory and she saw Eve lying there, but whether it was for herself, or for the dead android, or at this further evidence of what her few ill-chosen words had led to, I couldn't say.

'She was my only friend once,' Hr'oln said, 'and I think I have need of a friend again. We will work together to repopulate the planet.' She gestured round her at the scientific apparatus and the dodo pen. 'After all, no one knows better how this all works.'

'You could maybe rewire the "murderous scheming cow" circuit, though,' I suggested. But you couldn't really blame Hr'oln for what Eve had become, any more than you could blame Eve herself. After all that Hr'oln had lost…

And now the museum had gone too. 'No one will ever see an aye-aye again,' I said. 'Or a passenger pigeon, or a three-striped box turtle. No one without a time machine, anyway.'

'Nothing lasts forever,' the Doctor said, gazing into the distance. And then he focused again, and grinned. 'Well, except the dodo…'

Something struck me. 'Hang on, I know about cloning. You only get an exact copy, you can't propagate a species by it. Eve only had one of each kind. There won't be any boy Dorotheas.'

'True,' the Doctor agreed, sighing. He drew something out of his pocket, which I recognised as the feather from Dorothea he'd used to track us to the lab. Then he drew something out of his other pocket. The original dodo feather that had brought the TARDIS to the museum in the first place. 'Looks like it belongs to a boy to me,' he said.

Woo! I gave him a hug. Then I thought back to all those genetics lectures again and let go. 'Oi, you are talking to a medical student here, and I know you can't clone from a feather. You're just trying to make me feel better.'

'Martha, this is the future! Just accept that they can do things.' He looked suddenly serious. 'I don't do white lies.'

I believed him. 'Sorry,' I said, and hugged him again.

'And who knows how many other samples might just happen to drop out of my pockets…' he said, as he unlocked the TARDIS door. 'Hang on, pockets, that reminds me…'

He reached into his jacket and pulled out the *I-Spyder* guide, but I didn't hold out a hand for it. 'All the stuff I've seen,' I said, 'and I haven't got anywhere near enough points for a certificate. I think it's impossible.'

The Doctor grinned. 'Oh, I think there's one elusive specimen that you might be able to track down…' He scrolled through the index and pointed out an entry.

I laughed. 'Are they joking?'

He shook his head. 'No, just leaping to the wrong conclusion from the evidence.'

I did the sums. And couldn't believe it, because I was still a point short.

So the Doctor pointed out another entry, and I smiled. 'Of course!'

And then I smiled again, because this really was the end of the story. Well, apart from one last goodbye…

The Doctor was inside the TARDIS. Martha stood in the doorway, holding Dorothea. 'So… you must have had pets on board the TARDIS before, right?' she said hopefully.

The Doctor thought for a moment. 'You never met Mickey, did you?' Then he smiled and shook his head. 'Being apart from your own kind for ever – that's quite a burden to bear, you know.' He looked straight at her. 'However much you're loved.'

Martha held his gaze for a few moments, then dropped her eyes to Dorothea. 'Right,' she said reluctantly. She walked over to the pen, and lowered the bird inside. Without a backward glance, it trotted off to join its fellows. After a few moments, it was lost among the crowd. Martha, staring wistfully at the dodo throng, tried to pretend she knew which one was Dorothea. But, really, she didn't. So she thought instead of the future, of the planet where a dead species would live again. Then she thought of the past, of the last dodo that had been, to her, the first dodo; no longer doomed to a choice between a lonely life or a lonely death – and hoped that it was happy, wherever it was.

TIME LORD

Dominus temporis

Location: worldwide

The Time Lord is a rare bipedal, bicardial mammal. It frequently mingles with herds of Homo sapiens, but can be distinguished from them by its unique physiology and distinctive fearless behaviour. It is between approximately 1.5 and 2 metres in height, and can have white, black, brown or blond hair. It is most commonly found in Europe, especially the United Kingdom.

Addendum:

It has been suggested that the Time Lord is of non-terrestrial origin. However, sightings spanning several millennia indicate that, even if it did not originate on Earth, it should now be classified as an immigrant species.

I-Spyder points value: 8963400

Creature	Points
Dodo	800
Megatherium	500
Paradise parrot	500
Velociraptor	250
Mountain gorilla	500
Aye-aye	900
Siberian tiger	600
Kakapo	900
Indefatigable Galapagos mouse	1500
Stegosaurus	500
Triceratops	550
Diplodocus	600
Ankylosaurus	650
Dimetrodon	600
Passenger pigeon	100
Thylacine	250
Black rhinoceros	300
Mervin the missing link	23500
Tau duck	5
Chicken	4
Red-eared slider	40
Chinese three-striped box turtle	350
Forest dragonfly	150
Phorusrhacos	450
Steller's sea cow	1000
Sabre-toothed tiger	500
Megalosaurus	600
Time Lord	8963400
Subtotal	**8999999**

She was tired, so tired, and scared, and hopeless, but still she tried to run. It was no good. The leaf-animals were both calm and fast, and seemed to be in front of her whatever way she turned. Suddenly she felt pressure round her waist, and she was raised from the ground. This was it; this was when she went the same way as her babies and her mate – but she didn't give up, she desperately tried to turn her head, knowing her giant beak, hooked and sharp, was her greatest weapon against these soft, fleshy creatures.

Had she been less scared, she might have realised the difference between the gentle, soothing noises these creatures made and the harsh, cruel cries of the death-dealers. But fear had consumed her now.

One creature said: There's no need to be scared.

The other creature said: We're not going to hurt you.

The first said: I'm sorry. I'm so sorry about what's happened. But at least we can save you.

He lifted a small, square device that was like nothing

she had ever seen before, and held it before her… And suddenly she was in the same place, but it was different, so different. She was no longer being held, she was back on the ground, and she stumbled backwards in shock as some of the trees flashed out of existence and others shot up in the air, instantaneously tall. She had an impression of creatures like the leaf-animals lying down on the sands, with dark, flat objects covering their eyes, or raising containers of brightly coloured water to their minuscule fleshy beaks. Beyond them were bizarre structures, wider than a hundred trees, smooth and flat and shooting high into the sky, with tall creatures walking out of holes in their bases.

And then, in an instant, it all changed again.

The fleshy creatures had gone. So had the flat structures, and the too-tall trees. Now the trees looked even shorter than before…

This was all too much for her to take. Somewhere inside she felt relief that she was free from the clutches of the frightening creatures, but she was still suffering from the shock of seeing her fellows killed, and the exhaustion of the chase. Temporarily safe she may have been, but she was still alone, and still scared.

There were bushes nearby, not ones that she remembered, but that hardly mattered. She backed into them, hiding herself from the outside world. For a while she held herself upright, alert for any threat, then gradually she sank down to the floor and, finally, her eyes shut. Tired and alone, she slept.

When she awoke, she was no longer tired.

And she was no longer alone.

She pushed her way out of the bushes, her tiny wings flapping in delight. They had returned! Escaped, somehow! Then she stopped, puzzled. They were of her kind, but they were not her own people, they were strangers.

Slower, but still cautiously happy, she carried on towards them. She got a few curious glances, but they seemed pleased to meet her, greeting her as a new friend. One in particular gave an enthusiastic squawk of welcome, and she returned it with gusto. She was not yet ready to consider a new mate, but maybe one day… Maybe one day she would even have a baby again. There were no signs of the grunting things – her baby could grow up in safety.

But the most important thing was, she was no longer alone.

The last dodo waddled forwards, towards the future.

HUMAN

Homo sapiens

Location: Europe, Asia, Africa, North America, South America, Australia

The human is a bipedal mammal that walks upright. It is mainly hairless with only a few patches of hair, the main one being on its head. Its smooth skin ranges from a pale pinky-white to a deep black. The male human is on average taller and heavier than the female. It is the only species on Earth to voluntarily clothe itself.

As of publication, the human is still abundant on Earth.

I-Spyder points value: 2

Creature	Points
Dodo	800
Megatherium	500
Paradise parrot	500
Velociraptor	250
Mountain gorilla	500
Aye-aye	900
Siberian tiger	600
Kakapo	900
Indefatigable Galapagos mouse	1500
Stegosaurus	500
Triceratops	550
Diplodocus	600
Ankylosaurus	650
Dimetrodon	600
Passenger pigeon	100
Thylacine	250
Black rhinoceros	300
Mervin the missing link	23500
Tau duck	5
Dong tao chicken	4
Red-eared slider	40
Chinese three-striped box turtle	350
Forest dragonfly	150
Phorusrhacos	450
Steller's sea cow	1000
Sabre-toothed tiger	500
Megalosaurus	600
Time Lord	8963400
Human	2
Subtotal	9000001

This is to certify that

MARTHA JONES

has obtained the rank of

ARACHNID FIRST CLASS

with an I-Spyder points total of

9,000,001

signed

Big Chief I Spyder

Also available from BBC Books
featuring the Doctor and Rose
as played by Christopher Eccleston and Billie Piper:

DOCTOR·WHO

THE CLOCKWISE MAN
by Justin Richards

THE MONSTERS INSIDE
by Stephen Cole

WINNER TAKES ALL
by Jacqueline Rayner

THE DEVIANT STRAIN
by Justin Richards

ONLY HUMAN
by Gareth Roberts

THE STEALERS OF DREAMS
by Steve Lyons

Also available from BBC Books
featuring the Doctor and Rose
as played by David Tennant and Billie Piper:

DOCTOR·WHO

THE STONE ROSE
by Jacqueline Rayner

THE FEAST OF THE DROWNED
by Stephen Cole

THE RESURRECTION CASKET
by Justin Richards

THE NIGHTMARE OF BLACK ISLAND
by Mike Tucker

THE ART OF DESTRUCTION
by Stephen Cole

THE PRICE OF PARADISE
by Colin Brake

Also available from BBC Books
featuring the Doctor and Martha
as played by David Tennant and Freema Agyeman:

DOCTOR·WHO

Sting of the Zygons

by Stephen Cole

ISBN 978 1 84607 225 3

UK £6.99 US $11.99/$14.99 CDN

The TARDIS lands the Doctor and Martha in the
Lake District in 1909, where a small village has been
terrorised by a giant, scaly monster. The search is on
for the elusive 'Beast of Westmorland', and explorers,
naturalists and hunters from across the country are
descending on the fells. King Edward VII himself is
on his way to join the search, with a knighthood for
whoever finds the Beast.

But there is a more sinister presence at work in the Lakes
than a mere monster on the rampage, and the Doctor
is soon embroiled in the plans of an old and terrifying
enemy. As the hunters become the hunted, a desperate
battle of wits begins – with the future of the entire world
at stake...

Wooden Heart

by Martin Day

ISBN 978 1 84607 226 0

UK £6.99 US $11.99/$14.99 CDN

A vast starship, seemingly deserted and spinning slowly in the void of deep space. Martha and the Doctor explore this drifting tomb, and discover that they may not be alone after all…

Who survived the disaster that overcame the rest of the crew? What continues to power the vessel? And why has a stretch of wooded countryside suddenly appeared in the middle of the craft?

As the Doctor and Martha journey through the forest, they find a mysterious, fogbound village – a village traumatised by missing children and prophecies of its own destruction.

DOCTOR·WHO

Creatures and Demons

by Justin Richards

ISBN 978 1 84607 229 1

UK £7.99 US $12.99/$15.99 CDN

Throughout his many adventures in time and space, the Doctor has encountered aliens, monsters, creatures and demons from right across the universe. In this third volume of alien monstrosities and dastardly villains, *Doctor Who* expert and acclaimed author Justin Richards describes some of the evils the Doctor has fought in over forty years of time travel.

From the grotesque Abzorbaloff to the monstrous Empress of the Racnoss, from giant maggots to the Daleks of the secret Cult of Skaro, from the Destroyer of Worlds to the ancient Beast itself… This book brings together more of the terrifying enemies the Doctor has battled against.

Illustrated throughout with stunning photographs and design drawings from the current series of *Doctor Who* and his previous 'classic' incarnations, this book is a treat for friends of the Doctor whatever their age, and whatever planet they come from…

The Inside Story

by Gary Russell

ISBN 978 0 56348 649 7

£14.99

In March 2005, a 900-year-old alien in a police public call box made a triumphant return to our television screens. *The Inside Story* takes us behind the scenes to find out how the series was commissioned, made and brought into the twenty-first century. Gary Russell has talked extensively to everyone involved in the show, from the Tenth Doctor himself, David Tennant, and executive producer Russell T Davies, to the people normally hidden inside monster suits or behind cameras. Everyone has an interesting story to tell.

The result is the definitive account of how the new *Doctor Who* was created. With exclusive access to design drawings, backstage photographs, costume designs and other previously unpublished pictures, *The Inside Story* covers the making of all twenty-six episodes of Series One and Two, plus the Christmas specials, as well as an exclusive look ahead to the third series.